Dear Matthew,

I hope you come –
Auntie Robbo as much as I
do! May she continue
to inspire us all – God
knows we need it!

Lots of love,
Rebecca
xxx

Auntie Robbo

by

Ann Scott Moncrieff

Scotland Street Press
EDINBURGH

Published by Scotland Street Press 2019

Copyright © Ann Scott Moncrieff
Introduction Copyright © Lesley Findlay

First published by The Viking Press, New York 1941
First published in Great Britain by Constable and Co Ltd 1959
Then by The Bodley Head Ltd 1985

This edition in 2019 by
Scotland Street Press
Edinburgh
www.scotlandstreetpress.com
Cover Design by Theodore Shack
Illustrations by Christopher Brooker
ISBN: 978-1-910895-14-6
Typeset in Scotland by Theodore Shack
Printed and bound in Poland

Introduction

Ann Scott Moncrieff
Remembered

'A native of Orkney, she carried with herself always an island freshness...' So wrote Colm Brogan.

She was born Agnes Shearer on 11th January, 1914 in Orkney, though she later changed her name to Ann. Her father, John Shearer, was a tailor in Kirkwall: her mother, Jeannie Moir Murison, was a daughter of the manse but died when Agnes was ten. She grew up in and around Kirkwall, attended Kirkwall Academy, and served her apprenticeship as a journalist on the Orcadian. At eighteen she left Orkney for London, where she worked as a journalist in Fleet Street, and where she met George Scott Moncrieff. A glorious summer was spent camping and swimming round the north coast of Skye with friends. They became engaged, though she refused to marry til she was twenty. Something of her personal impact can be found in Death's Bright Shadow, a novel her husband wrote years later.

She gave up a course in archeology at Edinburgh University; they were married in 1934 and went to live near Stobo, Peebleshire, in a cottage which was let in return for work on the farm. That first year George made only £8 by his writing, but his wife did better. During the summer she finished her first book for children, Aboard the Bulger, and the following year her second, The White Drake and Other Stories.

When Eric and Marjory Linklater came out to see them, they were shown the cottage: one room down and one up with just room for a bed.

'And where do you keep your clothes?' Marjory asked.

'We wear them,' replied Ann with dignity.

She must have looked very young, for the local School Inspector came round to ask George why she was not attending school.

Among friends and colleagues at this time were John R. Allen, Sir James Fergusson, Robert Garioch, Tom MacDonald, Hector MacIver, Hugh MacDairmid and Moray McLaren. George and Ann were part of this group of writers and thinkers before and during the war who were later dubbed 'the Scottish Renaissance.'

They moved to Temple, Midlothian, where George wrote Tinkers Wind and The Lowlands of Scotland. Ann was contributing regularly to newspapers and magazines and many of her short stories date from this time. Correspondence with her brother-in-law, Charlie, reflects the apprehensions of three perceptive young people at the edge of Europe in 1938.

When a baby girl, Lesley, was born, their first home was a white cottage half-way between Dalwhinnie and Laggan, standing end-on to the rough road. They walked across high moors, skated on grey frozen lochs and in summer bathed in the burns. In autumn the stags would come down and roar around a clump of pines hard by the house and Ann could not persuade her daughter they were not lions. A brother, Michael was born during a blizzard in 1940. Some months later after due consideration, Ann telephoned her husband who was in Edinburgh to say she was going to become a Catholic. He wrote to his parents apologizing for breaking this shocking news to them, then he stormed north to argue. A day later he wrote again asking his parents to try and forgive her. In a third letter he tells them that he has decided to join her.

They moved to Haddington and their second son Gavin was born. But it was there that the news came through first that George's older bother Colin, had been killed in the desert, and then news of the younger Charlie's death in the Fleet Air Arm in Trinidad. Ann wrote:

'Noo words ar a' tae smoosh

And argument's in bruck...'

But the words had to go on. From 1940 to 1945 George edited the New Alliance, a quarterly periodical, which was a joint Irish and Scottish venture. It published political and historical comment, reviews, short stories and poems.

Contributors included Ann, J.F. Hendry, Frank O' Connor, Morley Jamieson and Robert McLellan. Jack B. Yeats did some of the illustrations. J.M. Reid's notable history of Scotland, later published as The Scots Tragedy, was first written for it, as were his perspicacious political articles on Europe and America. Many of Edwin Muir's poems were first published in the New Alliance.

During the first year of the war Auntie Robbo was rejected by Methuen, but it was accepted and published by Viking in America. However the complimentary copies of the book which were dispatched by ship, were torpedoed as they crossed the Atlantic. Meanwhile in London most of the copies of Aboard the Bulger also The White Drake were bombed in the publisher's cellars in Paternoster Row.

But Ann was increasingly unwell: battling ill health, the exigencies of looking after a young family in war-time and writing to deadlines. Letters to an old school friend, Hannah, in Orkney, throw light on those days, or nights.

> It is 20 past six in the morning and the reason for writing to you at this stricken hour, is that I've been up all night writing a broadcast, and so think it hardly worth and so on and so on. I'm a gey busy woman as I'm sure you are yoursel'. Hence the long gap between butter and noo; in fact just so long as the butter lasted if you see what I mean. Saw the last scrap on the plate this morning. 'Before this beautiful bountiful butter is perished, completely consumed,' says I, 'I'll write to me

old friend Hannah of the red hair, the good old Hannah. The never-fading, always working Hannah of the ham-bones.' Lass you can get tight on merely sitting up all night, or is this merely a reaction to BBC English? Oh, Hannah! Oh World! Oh Life! Oh would I were in Marston kitchen wi' my feet on the range singing psalms. But that was another day. You mind?

She died when she was only twenty-nine. A fitting tribute is paid to her in Edwin Muir's poem 'To Ann Scott Moncrieff'. Also by others including Morley Jamieson who wrote, 'Love for her was the medium of revelation, love of God and of human kind, in conversation, in journeying or merely in bathing her babies. Love…scorned the cautious compromise and stimulated thought and feeling among her friends whose company she would enter with relish as if all the time discoveries were about to be made and the conversation to unfold truths.'

The light of this spirit is reflected in these stories.

Lesley J. Findlay (daughter of Ann Scott Moncrieff)
Lochuanagan
2018

Auntie Robbo

CHAPTER ONE

Auntie Robbo liked to talk in the evening after dinner. That was why, when Hector had had his bath, he usually went down to the drawing-room in dressing-gown and slippers, and ate his supper of bread and jam and milk off one little tray while Auntie Robbo had her coffee off another. It was a cosy, friendly habit which they both enjoyed. It was supposed to be bad for Hector, for if they got on to an interesting subject they forgot all about bed. Auntie Robbo never sent anyone to bed.

One evening they sat together not saying very much, but content in their comfort and each other's company. It was early in March, and a great fire roared up the chimney in the wind. Rain tattled on the windowpanes, and the trees at the bottom of the garden were threshing and moaning as if they were a giant forest. The noise outside only enhanced the peace of the drawing-room; not a pompom of Auntie Robbo's plush curtains stirred in the storm. And all her furniture and flowered china and bits of silver and satin cushions glowed and winked in the firelight.

Hector sat on the fender, but the heat soon edged him onto the rug - the rug was a woolly white sheepskin one, warm and soft, delicious to dig the bare toes into. Hector dug his in and munched the last of his bread and jam, then he curled over like a comfortable cat, blinking up at Auntie Robbo.

He thought that she was looking nice tonight, the very picture of what an old lady should be. She was sitting up very straight and dignified in her winged armchair. Her hair was snowy and strained neatly into a bun at the nape of her neck. She wore a black satin gown which flowed in ample sober folds down over her shoes. Her hands lay still as doves on her tight-corseted stomach. A most proper and placid old lady. That's what you or I would have said. But Hector knew better. He knew his aunt was only sitting still and peaceful because of the good big dinner she had eaten, and her hands were folded not in piety but over the fullness of her stomach. Auntie Robbo was in fact thinking of the duckling and roast potatoes and claret and vanilla pudding that reposed beneath them. She sighed, a gentle satisfied sigh.

There's no denying Auntie Robbo was rather a gay old lady, frivolous in some ways. Take the number of ornaments she wore - little gold rings in her ears, a ruby pendant, two diamond birds flying across her bosom, an embroidered pocket, buckles on her shoes, and any number of rings and bracelets. Hector thought them all very pretty, but sometimes he wished she wouldn't wear quite so many. They were always falling off and getting lost.

He gazed up at her now, at her broad good-natured brown face and the creases that had come on it with so much smiling; and he pondered, as he often had before, whether the soul of his aunt had not been taken possession of by some goblin from the hills.

She grinned down at his serious face, and poured herself some coffee.

'I often think, Hector, living with me has made you old before your time.' She leaned forward to drop a spoonful of the little brown pebbles of coffee-sugar into his hand.

'M-m-m,' was all Hector said, crunching. He sometimes thought so himself, for Auntie Robbo's antics were hard to keep pace with, and it was difficult to stop her when she was going too far and too fast. That was Hector's job.

Hector was eleven, Auntie Robbo was eighty-one. She was not his aunt, nor even his great-aunt; she was his great-grand-aunt, and they got on as well together as any two people possibly could.

'But it's true, Hector. You're becoming quite aged.' Auntie Robbo wagged a ringed finger. 'Now isn't it about time you went to some school or other - ?' Her voice had risen to an affected shriek, for this was the way her niece Mrs. Agnew talked when she came to visit them.

'And made friends with other boys of my own age,' finished

Hector in the same tone.

She burst out laughing.

'And learned to play the game.'

'Cricket,' said Hector. 'With shiny bats and balls.'

'One ball and one bat,' she corrected him. 'You see how ignorant you are.'

'Very well, ma'am. I'll get on the bus at the end of the road tomorrow. They tell me there's some very good schools in Edinburgh.'

'Now don't be wilful. Have some more sugar and leave off teasing me.'

Hector took a handful of sugar, grinning.

'No, but I wasn't altogether in fun,' she went on. 'I mean when we started something ... what was it that put me in mind of poor Anna Agnew? Now what was it?'

But Hector had rolled over and closed his eyes against the firelight. He was never much interested in Mrs. Agnew.

Auntie Robbo prodded him with her toe gently and absent-mindedly, as if he had been a fat pet dog. Her brow was knitted in thought. It was a few moments before it cleared.

'That's it!' she cried, giving Hector a sharp dig in the with her toe. With a little yelp he sat up.

'It's on account of my not wearing this for so long,' said Auntie Robbo, feeling in the embroidered pocket which hung at her waistband. 'You know I made this pocket, Hector, when I was quite a girl. Look, the daisies are done with real gold thread. Isn't it clever? I don't believe I've ever sewn anything since. One can't do everything in this life. Now just look what

I found when I was dressing tonight.' She held up a letter between her thumb and forefinger. 'It must have come more than a month ago.' She opened her eyes wide and stared at the letter with some distaste, as if it were a fly in her soup or someone creating a scene at a dinner-party. Hector stared too.

'Is it an important letter?' he asked, impressed by her manner.

'I didn't think so at the time,' she explained, 'or I would have mentioned it. I just sort of skimmed through it. You know how one does. But when I read it again this evening, I felt it must be of some importance. It's from your stepmother.'

'Oh,' said Hector, and then added: 'I thought I was an orphan.'

'Now don't be stupid. Of course you are. Both your parents are dead - therefore you're an orphan. But you knew you had a stepmother, didn't you? I'm sure I must have mentioned it. When your father went abroad the last time - you were hardly crawling then - well, he got married to a woman he met in Egypt. He was ill even then and he died very shortly afterwards.'

'You *have* told me the story before,' said Hector. 'The woman was very beautiful.'

'Did I tell you that?' asked Auntie Robbo, looking anxious. 'You know, I've never heard what she was like really. But I imagine she must have been very beautiful, don't you? Or perhaps only very kind. However, we'll soon be able to judge for ourselves.'

'Are we going to see her?' asked Hector.

'Yes. She wants to come here. I was just going to tell you. It's all in the letter.'

'Read it to me,' said Hector.

Auntie Robbo shook out the letter, which was written on thin, tissuey paper in thin, sloping writing. 'Poof!' she said. 'It smells.' A thin odour of violets clung to the paper.

'Dear Miss Sketheway,' she read,

'You will no doubt be surprised to hear from me after all these years, but you wrote such kind letters at the time of my marriage and the death of my dear husband that I feel I can appeal to you in any difficulty. I have been ill lately; the climate is very trying. The doctors have ordered me to England - for six months at least, they say. I dare say it will make all the difference but I feel rather sad about it, as I have no longer any ties in the dear country - that is, unless I may count you as such. I hope I may. When I have settled my affairs in London, I mean to buy a car and tour the country a little. I should like to come north and pay you a visit. Naturally I am longing to see Hubert's son, my stepson. How much I have heard about him in the dear dead past! And what plans Hubert had for his future! We must have some long talks about him when we meet. I sail from here on Wednesday, and hope to be with you on the 10th of April in time for tea.

'Yours sincerely,

'Merlissa Benck Murdoch.'

Auntie Robbo sighed when she had finished. It wasn't a very promising letter. 'What d'you think?' she asked Hector.

Hector was pulling wool out of the rug. 'Was my father's name Hubert?' he said.

'No, of course it wasn't. It was Robert, after me. Dear me, I didn't notice that. It must be her writing - no, there it is, plain as can be - Hubert, not Robert. How strange! Maybe it was her pet name for him.'

'Or maybe she's forgotten. I think she's horrid. All stepmothers are horrid.'

'Now we mustn't be hasty, Hector. After all, she wasn't married to him that long. I really think perhaps we ought to have her here. Remember, we don't have many relations, and they all seem to have quarrelled with us. She may be very nice, you know. Besides, your father might have wished it.'

Auntie Robbo jumped out of her chair and strode up and down the room, her black skirts swishing against the furniture as she passed. She ran a hand through her hair and sent a cascade of hairpins onto the hearth rug.

'Do *you* want to see her?' she cried.

Hector was picking up hairpins. 'Well, she might be an Egyptian. If she was that I'd like to see her very much.'

'Of course, that's it,' cried Auntie Robbo. 'That might account for the letter. She doesn't know the language well; she says she has no ties in England. Look at that handwriting - there's Egyptian handwriting for you.'

Hector said it did look Egyptian. 'And Merlissa Benck is a queer kind of name.'

'Coffee-coloured, do you think?' said Auntie Robbo hopefully. 'With hair done in oil?'

'Lots of oil,' Hector agreed.

'Think of the camels -'

'Deserts -'

'The bazaars -'

'Mirages -'

'Date palms -'

'Arab ponies -'

'Think of the meals she must have eaten, living in little silk striped tents.'

'Think of the stories she'll be able to tell us.'

Auntie Robbo's eyes sparkled. If there was one thing she liked better than to talk after dinner, it was to be told a good story; hers and Hector's had been rather drying up lately.

'M-m-m,' said Auntie Robbo. 'I love Egypt. To think that I've passed it six times - or near it - and never been ashore.'

'A real Egyptian will be able to tell us everything,' said Hector enthusiastically.

'Of course,' she cried. 'That settles it then.'

And while Hector fell asleep on the sheepskin rug and dreamed it was Sahara's burning sands, Auntie Robbo sat down at her writing-desk and dashed off a warm welcoming letter to Merlissa Benck.

CHAPTER TWO

Nethermuir was the name of Auntie Robbo's house. It was about twelve miles from Edinburgh at the foot of the hills, and had a wide view over flat lowland moor to the city and the river Forth. It was a square squat house with modest-sized windows. And it was clothed, all but its roof, in a neat jacket of ivy. It had a white wooden porch, and in front of the dining-room and drawing-room windows two white summer seats made of curly iron, and in the middle of its garden an enormous white flagstaff. You really noticed these things before the modest house - they were so staringly white. Auntie Robbo had them painted every spring; she said they made the place look shipshape.

The hills rose directly behind the house, at first in long shaggy waves of turf and then in steeps of heather. You had to start climbing as soon as you got out of the back door. A burn ran down past the house; Auntie Robbo owned the lochan from which it rose about a mile higher up. Walking over the hills was a favourite ploy with her and Hector.

One wet April afternoon they had been out since lunchtime climbing higher and higher and every now and then stopping while Auntie Robbo rested on a shooting-stick and admired the view. Not that there was much view: only the rain clouds settling low on the moor and the smudged outline of the Pentland Hills. Spring was in the air. The wet wind fanned their cheeks and whipped raincoats about their legs. It was delicious to feel the ground give squelchily beneath them and to know that it was alive and springing with the new green of the year.

On one of these halts Auntie Robbo pointed down to the main road; a car was creeping along it. From their height it looked like a fussy blue beetle.

'Look at that thing!' she said. Auntie Robbo had great scorn for most products of the machine age. 'It doesn't go so fast, for all you say, Hector. There's nothing to beat a good turn-out of horse and gig.'

'It's because we're so high up,' said Hector. 'I bet it's going forty miles an hour.'

'Poof!'

'Easily - perhaps fifty.'

'Well, why isn't it past and away down the road by this time? It ought to have gone in a flash.' Auntie Robbo was triumphant, until she saw the reason for the car's slowness.

For at that moment it nosed round off the road, up the drive, and in through their own white gate.

'Visitors!' she gasped.

'Shall we run?' suggested Hector.

'No use,' she said resignedly, not without relief. 'We're too high. Let's just wait here till they go away.'

Visitors were few and far between at Nethermuir; Auntie Robbo and Hector did nothing to encourage them. For one thing afternoon tea - an anglo-dandified habit, Auntie Robbo called it - broke up their afternoon and disorganized the rest of their meals. Auntie Robbo never drank tea at any time and the act of having to pour it out for other people made her very cross, so cross that she would hardly say a word to her guests. Then Hector had to do all the entertaining, which consisted mainly in handing plates of bread and butter and cake, and submitting to pats on the head and advice about the school he must go to. No, visitors weren't popular with Auntie Robbo and Hector.

Still, they quite welcomed this strange car, since they were safe from its occupants. And it was pleasant, drawing breath high up on the wet hillside, to speculate who it might be.

'The minister?' said Auntie Robbo.

'No, he was here for dinner last week. That ought to have settled him. Besides he comes on his bicycle,' said Hector. 'It might be that soldier with the red moustaches - you know, he told us stories.'

'Cousin Bill? No, he's in India.'

'Mrs. Agnew.' Hector pulled a face.

'No, she doesn't like us now.'

They had exhausted their list of possibilities.

'Whoever it is,' said Hector, 'they're waiting. They haven't come out again.'

'Oh, dear. Shall we start going down very slowly? I suppose we ought.'

They started downhill at a snail's pace, looking anxiously for the reappearance of the car; but it remained parked out of sight in front of the house. Soon Hector was racing ahead, plunging and leaping down the slope. Once he tripped and curled over and over in the drenched heather. He waited for Auntie Robbo at the top of the back garden, and they went soberly together towards the house.

'I hope Amy has given them tea,' muttered Auntie Robbo, 'then I shan't have to pour out. Now, s-s-sh.' She lifted the sneck of the back door and they crept into the lobby.

Amy bustled out of the kitchen. She was a very neat and competent parlour-maid. She had come to them from Mrs. Agnew's and she had, according to Auntie Robbo, 'no sense of humour.' She did in fact disapprove of Auntie Robbo and Hector; especially Hector - she wasn't so afraid of him.

She looked down her nose now when Auntie Robbo, grimacing and waving wet arms in the direction of the drawing-room, hissed: 'Who is it and what do they want?'

'Who is it?' hissed Hector, hopping from one leg to the other.

Amy replied loudly and primly: 'Miss Benck has arrived, ma'am. She's having tea in the drawing-room.'

'Oh!' Their faces went blank with horror.

'Merlissa Benck! Bless me, Hector, she's come. It's the Egyptian stepmother. Is this really the tenth of the month? I would never have believed it. How awful of us!'

'Shall I get the spare room ready, ma'am?' asked Amy. 'Yes, do.'

'Is she black?' asked Hector. He had begun to hop again in excitement. Amy gave him a withering look, and turned on her heel.

'Come on, Hector.' Auntie Robbo swept forward, shedding wet garments as she passed through the hall and into the drawing-room.

Hector followed more slowly, taking time over peeling off his raincoat. He liked to savour the excitement of meeting Merlissa Benck in advance. He went and washed his hands. An Egyptian stepmother! That was something to get excited about. He applied a brush to his rain-soaked hair with great enthusiasm. Then, plastered and neat and clean, he walked towards the drawing-room, smiling in anticipation.

As soon as he rounded the big painted screen that guarded the door, he stopped dead. The smile remained fixed on his face, but stupidly, and his legs would not carry him forward.

'So this is little Hector!' trilled a high feminine voice. A rush of steps from the hearth rug and he found himself clutched to an ample fur-clad bosom; it smelled of dead animal and potpourri and moth balls.

'But of course it is, the darling - the very image of his father.'

Hector found himself pushed out at arm's length and surveyed; Merlissa Benck's eyes were cold and round and yellowish-grey, like a couple of Scots pebbles, the uglier kind of Scots pebbles, or perhaps the kind that is made uglier because of their setting. Hector stared back into these eyes as if he had been a rabbit come face to face with a stoat. Not that Merlissa Benck was like a stoat really; she was certainly not like an Egyptian. She was a fat dumpy sort of a woman; she seemed to be short of breath; her face was round and creeshy and white - whiter than the back of a floury bannock. She wasn't even healthily tanned. In fact, the Egyptian sun, far from improving her face as might have been expected, seemed to have drained away all its natural colour, leaving it flat, insipid, dead white. She had glistening white china teeth. They were set in rubber-red sockets; they weren't pretty. She had some yellow hair, very nicely curled.

Hector gulped, trying to swallow his horrible disappointment. 'How do you do?' he managed to say at last.

And Merlissa Benck again hugged him, and pushed him from her, and hugged him again.

'Perhaps you'd like to finish tea,' came Auntie Robbo's voice.

Hector was released.

'Oh, yes, of course,' said Merlissa Benck. 'I do love my tea. Aren't you having any?'

'Never touch the stuff,' said Auntie Robbo. She was standing in front of the fire, drying the bedraggled ends of her long tweed skirt. She swayed aggressively now. 'Never touch it. Tans the stomach.'

Hector looked hard at her. He could see she was going to be difficult. Of course she was disappointed too, but it was silly to be rude to Merlissa Benck - she might be quite nice really. He grabbed a plate of bread and butter and held it out to the guest.

'The cake, darling. Thank you. Yes, Miss Sketheway, I have heard it does that to some people,' said Merlissa Benck. 'At your age I suppose one has to be careful.'

Hector watched Auntie Robbo anxiously. She placed her broad freckled hands on her hips and visibly swelled with wrath. She looked twice as strong, twice as healthy as Merlissa Benck; no one would have taken her for twice as old, which she was. Still, thought Hector, there was no need to show off about it, not now anyway. And just as the pent-up abuse was about to burst from Auntie Robbo...

'Of course you're absolutely marvellous for your age, aren't you?' cooed Merlissa Benck. 'I can hardly believe you're over seventy.'

Auntie Robbo collapsed like a pricked balloon. She could not resist saying: 'Over eighty,' and then she bit her lip angrily.

Hector smiled at her. No one else would have dared to do such a thing at such a moment, but Auntie Robbo and Hector understood each other well. She smiled back, wryly and apologetically.

'Your stepmother is English, Hector,' she said. It was by way of a private explanation. Something in her tone nettled Merlissa Benck, though she couldn't think why. Surely it was a compliment she was being paid.

'Well, I have some good Scots blood in me too,' she laughed.

'Don't apologize,' said Auntie Robbo with a magnificent wave of her hand. 'Don't apologize.'

Merlissa Benck stopped in the act of biting her cake. She stared doubtfully at her hostess.

'We were expecting you to be different,' Hector hastened to say. Auntie Robbo could be very rude about the English. 'We made sure you would be Egyptian.'

'Coloured?' cried Merlissa Benck in a shocked voice, and she was so incensed that actually a little colour did creep into her cheeks.

'Yes,' said Auntie Robbo.

'A little coloured,' said Hector. 'By the sun, you know.'

Merlissa Benck laughed in a relieved voice; Hector laughed politely; Auntie Robbo laughed immoderately.

'Well,' said Merlissa Benck, 'I'm white and proud of it; white through and through - that's how you'll find me, Hector.' She patted him on the head.

There was a loud snorting explosion from Auntie Robbo's chair, a whisk of long skirts, and she had fled. 'Have some more tea,' said Hector to their startled guest.

CHAPTER THREE

'But why does she call herself Benck - Miss Benck?' asked Hector through a mouthful of bread and marmalade. 'Why isn't she a Mrs., and if she was married to my father, why isn't she Mrs. Murdoch?'

Auntie Robbo poured herself out some more coffee. She and Hector were alone at breakfast. Merlissa Benck had not come down yet. 'Does it matter?' she asked abstractedly, gazing out of the window at the grey soaking morning.

'Yes,' said Hector, frowning. 'It doesn't make sense.'

'Oh, well, perhaps she wants to marry again, or she's been left money under a Benck's will, or something like that.' Auntie Robbo plainly did not want to discuss their guest; Hector wondered what had happened in the drawing-room after he had gone to bed last night; he hoped Auntie Robbo had behaved herself. As a matter of fact, Auntie Robbo had behaved; that was what was making her feel a little old and depressed.

'Good morning, all,' said a bright voice, and there was Merlissa Benck smiling her china smile and looking even whiter than usual in the raw early air.

Auntie Robbo helped her to porridge, which she didn't eat, inquired how she had slept, and then suggested that Hector should take her for a walk during the morning and show her the neighbourhood.

'That would be lovely,' said the guest, looking unenthusiastically out of the window. 'But wouldn't it be better to wait till it clears up?'

'It will never clear up,' said Auntie Robbo firmly. 'Never. Not this day.'

Hector thought perhaps that it would be better to take Merlissa out of Auntie Robbo's way, so he said kindly: 'I've got heaps to show you. Do come. It's very nice outside once you're wet.'

Merlissa Benck brightened, gushing: 'Oh, you little darling. I'm just dying to see your domain.'

Hector looked a little puzzled. He had meant to take her simply a mile down the road to buy some black-striped balls at Nethermuir post-office, but now a somewhat more intricate walk seemed to be called for.

As soon as they left the house, Merlissa Benck began to chat confidentially to him.

'Now, Hector, you must tell me all about yourself. I'm

longing to know everything. Do you go into Edinburgh often?'

'Oh, no, hardly ever,' said Hector.

'Do you mean to say your aunt doesn't keep a car at Nethermuir?'

'We sometimes go in the bus.'

'You must come with me one day soon. You'd like that, wouldn't you?'

Hector smiled brightly.

'Doesn't your aunt go about at all? Doesn't she take you anywhere? Oh, I suppose she's getting too old for that sort of thing.'

'Well, yes, I suppose so. We have the ponies though. Sometimes we ride quite a long way. Easily as far as Edinburgh - only in the other direction. 'Way down that way.' Hector waved his hand southward over the hills.

'You ride? Your aunt rides?' Merlissa Benck's mouth gaped so that Hector feared her teeth might fall out; he distinctly heard them click into position as she recovered herself. 'It's quite preposterous in a woman of her age. Riding at eighty - or ninety - or whatever it is! Suppose anything was to happen when you were out alone with her. Suppose she had an accident - or heart failure.'

Hector looked puzzled. 'Well, I could save her,' he said at last. 'I could gallop for help. It would be better than if she was quite, quite alone.'

'Oh, how noble,' burst out Merlissa Benck. She put an arm round Hector's neck. 'But these are your most impressionable years. The shock might mar you for life. I do think your aunt is a most reckless woman. Selfish in some ways. Not at all the sort of person to be looking after young people.' Hector broke away from her uncomfortably.

'Mind your step here. We cross this burn and climb up it along that little path on the other side.'

The burn was in spate, plunging downwards in a brown yeasty mass; but it was a little shallow burn, really, and there was no need for Merlissa Benck to yell so loud when she slipped off one of the stepping-stones; nor to splash about wildly while she groped for the bank.

'It's all right,' shouted Hector. 'Only three inches.'

But he was all compunction when he had helped her ashore and saw how wet she was.

'Oh, I *am* sorry,' he said. 'But it was your own fault. Never mind. The heather will be wet higher up and now you'll never feel it.'

Merlissa Benck, recovering from her panic, gave her china smile and said shortly that it didn't matter. They began to climb up along the burn by a slippery mud sheep-track.

'Shouldn't you be doing lessons at this time, Hector?' panted Merlissa Benck after a while. 'I suppose your aunt gave you a holiday for me.'

'Oh, I suppose so,' Hector replied gaily. 'But we only do them on and off anyway.'

'What do you mean, on and off?' Her voice was sharp. She stopped in the path. Hector turned round. 'When we feel like it,' he said mildly.

Merlissa Benck's expression had become hard and eager; she was like a hound picking up an interesting scent; she panted for breath on the steep, windy hillside.

'I understood from your aunt that you had a tutor, a Mr. Mathison, the minister here. Surely he insists on regular hours.'

'Oh, yes, every Friday. He teaches us Latin.'

'Us?' breathed his stepmother.

'Auntie Robbo and me. She never learned any Latin when she was young. I say, you mustn't stand still in your wet feet. We must keep walking.'

Hector led the way up the path.

'But what about ... Hector, wait for me ... What about other subjects?'

'Oh, Auntie Robbo knows all about them. Sometimes we do sums. We keep account books, and history - lots of history; then afterwards we ride over the battlefields and go and look at the castles where the murders were done.'

Seeing Merlissa Benck's shocked expression, Hector explained seriously. 'Scottish history has a great many murders, you know.'

'I dare say,' said Merlissa Benck shortly. 'But I should have thought *British* history would have been more suitable for a boy of your age, indispensable in *my* opinion. England's story is a very great and noble one.'

'Yes,' said Hector. 'But then we couldn't ride to the battlefields, could we? I mean they were mostly fighting in places that didn't belong to them, weren't they?'

'Certainly not - at least unless it was for a very good cause.'

'Auntie Robbo says the causes won't bear looking into.'

'What other lessons have you?' asked Merlissa Benck in exasperation.

'Oh, Gaelic poetry. Auntie Robbo is frightfully good at that. She had a Gaelic nurse when she was young who had the second sight. Her name was Morag, and Morag's brother was a bard. Then let's see; we've done an awful lot of geography. Auntie Robbo has been three times to New Zealand and twice to South America and once to Italy, passing through France, and once to Norway. So we've done all these places very thoroughly. Oh, and French; we read French. This summer we're going to make a grand tour.'

'Whatever for?' cried Merlissa Benck.

'To finish my education,' replied Hector confidently.

'Nonsense!' but the wind flung the word back in her teeth. Merlissa Benck snapped her mouth tight on it.

Hector bounded ahead out of the gully through which the burn ran and onto a tableland of moor.

'Come on,' he shouted, and Merlissa Benck struggled after him.

A neat little lochan lay on the tableland and it was its brown, peaty waters that fed the burn.

'This is the Splash,' explained Hector. 'And we own all the land up to it. In the summer time we bring a boat up; it's in the stable loft now. The two ponies pull it - they're immensely strong. Now watch this -'

Hector pulled a scone out of his pocket and began

crumbling it, casting it on the water.

Merlissa Benck had regained her breath. 'Then I suppose you'll be going to school in the autumn when you and your aunt come back from this ... this so-called grand tour.'

'S-s-sh,' said Hector. 'You're a stranger, so you'd better keep low down behind me.' He began to whistle.

From the far side of the lochan a pair of wild ducks began to scutter across the water towards them.

'Hold your breath,' whispered Hector, strung up with excitement.

The wild ducks came closer, swimming carefully. Then the brown female dived right close in to gobble the bread, but the male one circled far out, cautious and aloof.

'Isn't he a beauty?' breathed Hector. 'They're not so tame this time of the year. Let's go now so as he can get some food as well. What would you like to see next?'

'I'd like to get out of this bog before I sink to my knees,' said Merlissa Benck with some asperity.

Hector stared at her.

'Oh,' he said in a subdued voice. 'There's a road over there.'

They plodded over to it in silence. It was a cart-track, a deep cutting between banks of heather. Water ran down the middle of it but there were comparatively dry patches on either side.

'This is better,' said Merlissa Benck, putting good humour back into her voice. 'Now do tell me about this school you're going to. You've no idea how interested I am.'

'I'm not going to school,' he said.

She gave a little cry of protest, and Hector, hurriedly so as not to hurt her feelings by explaining that he didn't want to go to school, added:

'You see, I haven't learned the proper things for the entrance examination.'

'You poor lamb. Of course not. I *quite* understand. But wonderful things can be done with a tutor, a *proper* tutor, I mean. Now suppose we got one for you right away, you could -'

But Hector ceased to listen. He had heard it all so often before over the drawing-room tea-table. By and by he began to jump dexterously from side to side over the water which flowed down the middle of the cart-track. When he heard Merlissa Benck's voice trail up in a question, he would turn and smile serenely; and if she still looked for an answer from him, he would say: 'Yes, that's right,' or 'Of course.'

Thus they passed down the hill, through the village, and along the main road. When they reached the white gate of Nethermuir, Merlissa Benck fell silent. She had pointed out fully the advantages of a public school education, the dullness of living at Nethermuir, the queerness of Auntie Robbo, and the brilliant career that lay in front of Hector if only he followed her advice. She was satisfied she had made a considerable impression upon Hector. Her eyes gleamed with triumph, even as she limped, dripping and exhausted, up the last few yards of the drive.

CHAPTER FOUR

After lunch Merlissa Benck was looking so wearied and wan ('With a white face like that,' said Auntie Robbo, 'you can hardly tell when it gets any whiter') that Auntie Robbo suggested that she should lie down in her room for the afternoon. She agreed quite thankfully.

'Perhaps you shouldn't have taken her up to the Splash, Hector,' said Auntie Robbo when she had left them. 'Not used to the climate. And Egypt's as flat as a plate. So is England for that matter. I expect the hill was too much for her.'

'She asked to see our domain.'

'Yes, isn't she funny? You can see the whole of it from the bathroom window. I don't know why she wanted to go tramping off in those high-heeled shoes.'

They both sighed. Merlissa Benck had hardly been a night

and a day in the house, yet all their placid life seemed to
be broken and upset. Instead of going on from one thing
to another leisurely, never thinking of what was going to
happen next, they found their day chopped into sections
and hours. Over all reigned the comfort and convenience of
Merlissa Benck. And it was very difficult to tell just what that
comfort and convenience *was*. It seemed to be quite different
from their idea of comfort and convenience.

'Never mind,' said Auntie Robbo, brightening. 'It's only
for a few more days. She won't be able to stand us longer.
Nobody ever does.'

She had got into her gardening boots and gloves, and they
went out together to the tool shed.

'I can't imagine what she came for,' said Auntie Robbo.
'Didn't we invite her? Now what was it that made us do that?'

'We thought she'd be an Egyptian and tell us stories.'

'Oh, yes, of course. And then she's your stepmother.'

Hector was bored with the subject of Merlissa Benck.
'Ground's a bit heavy today,' he said. 'Will we be doing the
seed boxes?'

'Yes, let's!' agreed Auntie Robbo, coming out of her
dwalm. And in a few minutes they were blissfully at work
with mould and sand and brightly coloured packets of seeds.
And their guest might have been back in Egypt, for all they
thought of her.

Merlissa Benck, on the other hand, spent the whole
afternoon thinking about them. Lying on her back in bed
with the blinds drawn against the horrid Scotch day, her

mind fairly buzzed with indignation against Auntie Robbo and with plans for the future of Hector.

'After all, I am his stepmother,' she mused. 'And that's a nearer relationship really than a great-grand-aunt. Great-grand-aunt, indeed! It's hardly decent. The old woman ought to be in her grave.' And her face lengthened as she thought that Auntie Robbo looked like living as long as she did herself. 'But I must get Hector away from here - and from her. Hubert would have wished it. I remember him telling me quite well that he thought Miss Sketheway queer in the head. Very Scots, he called her - that was his way of putting it. Dear Hubert - always so loyal.'

Merlissa Benck persisted in thinking of Hector's father as Hubert, although in fact his name was Robert. The truth was, just as Hector had guessed, she had forgotten his real name. But neither Auntie Robbo nor Hector had come near to guessing the reason why she had forgotten it. It was a very simple reason: Merlissa Benck had had two husbands since then. She had buried the last of them before leaving Egypt. No wonder she did not call herself Mrs. Murdoch, for in the ensuing ten years she had also been Mrs. Bishop and Mrs. Van der Post. Nowadays she preferred to be known by her maiden name of plain Miss Benck; it saved confusion and a lot of explanation.

For, strange to say, Merlissa Benck didn't enjoy the thought of having been married three times. It worried her. Somehow it wasn't *right*. It wasn't *respectable*. It made her sound like a sultan or a Mormon, and she never thought of herself like that. In fact, sometimes she would imagine she had never had any other name but Mrs. Bishop, at other times that of Mrs. Van der Post. She had rarely thought of herself as Mrs. Murdoch until lately, but now it was as if she had had no other husband than Hector's father; and that of course made Hector very near.

Merlissa Benck's mind worked in a funny way. The idea of Hector had been bobbing about in it ever since she had left Egypt. It had occurred to her how nice it would be to have a son - even if it were only a stepson - of that age. She was middle-aged, she was rich, she was lonely. And she had been married three times. A stepson like Hector was just what she wanted. To do Merlissa Benck justice, she hadn't set out with the deliberate intention of grabbing what she wanted. She hadn't come to stay at Nethermuir in order to lay hands on Hector. That had barely occurred to her. But now that she had seen Auntie Robbo and had seen Hector and had seen the kind of life they led, she realized that it was her duty to rescue him at all costs. It was her duty to adopt him, to send him to a good school, and to bring him up in the way he should go; and he would look after her when she was old, and inherit her money. It was a delightful thought.

Merlissa Benck lay back on her pillows, exulting, planning a rosy future. And if Hector had seen her then he might have thought that after all she resembled a stoat. Her little eyes gleamed, her long thin nose twitched, every now and then she ran the tip of her tongue greedily along her lips.

'It will be quite simple,' she thought, reverting to her first consideration of detaching Hector from Auntie Robbo, 'One has only to do one's duty.'

At that moment there was a knock at the door, and the parlour-maid entered with tea on a tray.

'Tea already, Amy?' said Merlissa Benck.

'Yes, ma'am, it's half-past four. I hope you're feeling better.'

'Yes, thank you, but I'll be glad of some tea. Is Miss Sketheway downstairs? Oh, I forgot, she doesn't have tea.'

'Miss Sketheway is in the garden, ma'am. She doesn't like to be disturbed, so I just took this up to you. I thought you'd like it here.'

Merlissa Benck felt slightly aggrieved, but she smiled brightly and said: 'It was very nice of you to remember me, Amy. I shall enjoy having it here.'

The parlour-maid was about to leave the room when Merlissa Benck called her back.

'You know, you're a very good parlour-maid, Amy. Ever since I came here, I've been struck by you.' Amy simpered.

'I don't want to appear curious,' went on Merlissa Benck, 'but I've often wondered how you came to be working here. I mean it's such a bleak, out-of-the-way place. If I've said to myself once, I've said it a dozen times: 'That's an uncommonly smart girl, not a *country* girl; or at least she's been trained in a much better - I mean bigger - household than this.''

'It is, ma'am,' replied Amy. 'I used to be with Mrs. Agnew in Edinburgh, that's Miss Sketheway's niece. She's a very great lady, quite a different sort of house, I can tell you. Mrs.

Agnew asked me to come here as a personal favour, when Miss Sketheway was wanting a new parlour-maid. She said the house needed somebody smart, and somebody who could keep an eye on Miss Sketheway for the family.'

'Really!' said Merlissa Benck, and her eyes protruded with interest.

But Amy, afraid that she had gone too far, hastened to say: 'I dare say they think she's getting too old. Of course I shan't stay here always - it's so lonely, like you say, ma'am, and then the cook here is no companion for a girl like me.' Amy pursed

her lips, and then bent forward confidentially: 'The bottle.'

'Indeed.'

'If it wasn't for Mrs. Agnew, I wouldn't stay another day. But then she's a great lady, and when Miss Sketheway dies - in the course of nature as we all must - I will be able to go back to her.'

'I quite understand, Amy,' said Merlissa Benck. 'I'm sure your reasons for staying here do you credit. Now what do you think of Master Hector? How do you think he's growing up? Remember he's my stepson and naturally I'm interested.'

Amy shook her head in a way that at once left Hector without a shred of character. She let out a slight despairing groan.

'Come now, I want to know the truth,' probed Merlissa Benck.

'He's never had a chance, as you might say,' began Amy, with a great show of reluctance. 'No schooling, no boys of his own age to knock the stuffing out of him. He's growing to be a regular little fiend, I can tell you, ma'am. Running about the countryside like a wild thing, and his great-grand-aunt that ought to be setting him an example running along with him, egging him on. And the lies, ma'am, you wouldn't believe the lies - the lies they tell each other. It's cruel to hear them on the lips of an innocent child....'

And so Amy flowed on, while Merlissa Benck sipped her tea, pursed her lips, and sighed at intervals: 'Just as I feared.'

At last she set down the cup. 'I don't know when I've enjoyed a cup of tea so much. Thank you, dear Amy.'

Amy, leaving the room with the tray, turned to give the guest a gratified smile.

From then on, she and Merlissa Benck were as thick as thieves.

CHAPTER FIVE

In the evening when Hector came down after his bath he found the drawing-room empty; he sat down cross-legged on the sheepskin rug in front of the fire and began his supper. From the dining-room, across the passage, came a murmur of conversation between Auntie Robbo and Merlissa Benck, still at dinner. By and by the murmur divided itself into two distinct voices, becoming shrill and staccato on the one hand and a deep growling grumble on the other. There seemed to be a bit of an argument going on. Hector listened apprehensively. However, he felt there was nothing he could do about it, and he went on eating stolidly. Now there came intervals of painful silence, and then the voices would break out again in their respective keys, as if both ladies had been drawing breath, glaring at each other across the table, and then bursting forth again.

During one of these pauses the dining-room door was snapped open and Auntie Robbo's voice came with great finality: 'I tell you the whole thing is ridiculous, quite ridiculous,' and presently she swept into the drawing-room ahead of Merlissa Benck.

Auntie Robbo was at her most magnificent, flushed and excited, anger adding fire to her brown cheeks and faded eyes. She was wearing one of her grandest evening dresses: a purple taffeta one nipped in at the waist, spread out into a fan-shaped train. It was festooned with bunches of net and white rosettes and from the corsage hung two twinkling tassels of diamonds. Auntie Robbo wore this confection right regally; she loved her clothes as she loved her food.

'Catch,' she said to Hector, tossing a little bunch of black grapes onto the rug beside him. 'They're very good this time, not a bit sour.'

Merlissa Benck came waddling in, looking like a ruffled and well-pecked hen; her face was harassed and moist. She sat down by the fire, crossed and uncrossed her plump legs, and shrilled with an affection of ease:

'So here you are, Hector. Having a nice simple supper by the fire while we two old ladies have been feasting next door.'

'Yes,' said Hector, eyeing the handkerchief which she was twisting and untwisting in her lap. He felt quite sorry for her.

Auntie Robbo began to pour out coffee. 'What do you think, Hector,' she said in her old calm voice, 'your stepmother thinks it would be nice to adopt you.'

Hector dropped his piece of bread jam-side down on the sheepskin rug, and for an instant his face was suffused with horror. Then he said blankly: 'Oh!' bending to pick up the bread.

'Just look what you've made him do!' cried Merlissa Benck. 'You quite startled the little chap. I should never have broken the news to him like that.'

Poor Hector stared at her now. 'It's not all settled, is it?' he gulped.

'No, no! Not quite. But it can be just as soon as you like, dear.' She darted a triumphant glance at Auntie Robbo, but Auntie Robbo was bent over the coffee tray.

'Black or white, Miss Benck?'

'Oh, white, if you please.' She was quite sure of herself now. She tucked the handkerchief away in her bag, and leaned forward confidentially to Hector. 'You see, it all began with our little conversation this morning. When I pointed out to your great-grand-aunt what a good thing it would be if you were to go to school and how anxious you yourself were for it, she wouldn't treat the matter seriously at all. She wouldn't even *discuss* schools with me. Now was that fair? So I just said - blunt is almost my middle name, as your poor father used to tell me - I just said: 'Very well, if you can't see your way to doing your duty by the boy, I will. I don't mind adopting him.''

Merlissa Benck leaned back, staring at Hector.

'That was very nice of you,' he managed to say.

She glowed at him.

'Yes, wasn't it?' said Auntie Robbo mildly. 'And she's got simply heaps and heaps of money, far more than me, all of which she will leave to you if you will become her adopted son.'

Hector looked at Merlissa Benck with a new respect. It seemed impossible that such a dull-looking person, wearing such ugly clothes, should have a lot of money.

'Your great-grand-aunt,' pursued Merlissa Benck, 'said that you were entirely free to choose for yourself. Of course she is your legal guardian, but I flatter myself that I can be something more to you - after all, I am not so very much older than you - more of a friend' - Merlissa Benck's voice became soft and blurred with emotion - 'and more of a mother.'

She stopped and looked at Hector. Hector shuffled uncomfortably and then he saw that there was no way out but the one way.

'Well, the truth is,' he said in a flat voice, 'I don't think I really want to go to school.'

He watched anxiously as Merlissa Benck's cheeks blew out, growing a pale lavender with rage. Auntie Robbo stirred her coffee noisily, saying in a benevolent helpless sort of voice: 'There you are, you see, Miss Benck.'

'It's preposterous,' shrilled Merlissa Benck. 'The boy isn't of an age to decide for himself. He doesn't realize how his future depends on it. Here he is wasting the best years of his life on a doting, selfish old woman - no, I won't apologize, I will speak the truth -'

'Yes, yes, do, please,' urged Auntie Robbo.

'Oh, you are impossible!' shouted Merlissa Benck, and bursting into tears she ran out of the room. They cocked their heads, listening to her sobbing all the way up the stairs and along the passage. A door slammed, and they turned slowly to look at each other in dismay.

Auntie Robbo brought out a big red handkerchief from a pocket in one of her lacy underskirts; she mopped her forehead. 'I couldn't help it, Hector. It wasn't my fault really.'

Hector jumped up and hugged her. 'I think you managed it very well,' he said. 'Here, have one of my grapes.'

Auntie Robbo chuckled. 'I didn't even have to play her. It was like lifting a salmon out in the off-season. All the same, it was the only thing to do.'

'I suppose it was. I *never* said I wanted to go to school, and what on earth made her think I would be adopted by her? Why, we hardly know her yet.'

'We've known her since yesterday, but it seems a great long while.'

'I think she's daft,' said Hector finally, rubbing a bit of jam into the sheepskin rug. 'Shall I get out the chessmen?'

'Yes, a nice quiet game,' agreed Auntie Robbo. 'That'll take our minds off our troubles.'

When the quaint carved red and white figures were arranged on the board, Auntie Robbo murmured: 'She can hardly want to stay after what's happened.'

Hector merely nodded, absorbed in his first move.

CHAPTER SIX

Whether Merlissa Benck wanted to stay on at Nethermuir or no, the next morning decided the question for her. It turned out she had to stay. When Auntie Robbo and Hector came down to breakfast they found Amy with an unnaturally long face and a very disapproving air.

'Miss Benck is confined to her bed, ma'am,' she sniffed. 'She's all of a doodah, and her temperature's rising.'

'How dreadful!' exclaimed Auntie Robbo, thinking only that Merlissa Benck's departure would now be postponed.

Amy went on sourly. 'It must have been the walk she took yesterday that's given her a chill, and her nerves are all to pieces. She was crying half the night, she told me.'

Hector and Auntie Robbo looked at each other in consternation.

'Oh, how dreadful!' repeated Auntie Robbo, and this time her voice was sincerely contrite.

'Poor Miss Benck,' said Hector. 'I hope she's not as bad as you think, Amy.'

'She's worse,' said Amy shortly. 'And no wonder.'

Auntie Robbo and Hector wriggled uncomfortably under her accusing eye. Then Auntie Robbo rallied. 'Well, have you sent for Doctor Mackenzie? We'd better do that at once. See that Miss Benck has everything she wants, and I'll come upstairs presently.'

'She doesn't want Doctor Mackenzie. She wants a nerve specialist from Edinburgh - here's his name.' Amy planked down a card on the table. 'And she said she'd rather not see anybody until she feels better.'

'Oh, very well,' said Auntie Robbo helplessly. 'Ring up his telephone number, and I'll get hold of this man for her.'

Auntie Robbo golloped up the last of her porridge and hurried out of the room after Amy. Hector toyed listlessly with his; his appetite seemed to have gone; it was another wet grey day and Merlissa Benck was a nervous wreck in the spare bedroom. But shortly Auntie Robbo came back, seeming almost her old cheerful self again. 'It's all right,' she said. 'He's coming down this morning. He seemed a charming man, quite charming. He said people from Egypt were often taken that way. Extraordinary, isn't it? Are you having this egg - no? Then I will.'

Hector could not get rid of his gloom so easily. 'Amy knows,' he said.

Auntie Robbo was quenched; she nodded and groaned, her mouth full of egg.

'We should have been kinder to Merlissa Benck,' said Hector, 'last night.'

Auntie Robbo nodded and groaned even more vehemently. She wiped her mouth. 'I know. It's awful. We must just try and be very good to her in future.'

They finished breakfast in depressed silence. Then Merlissa Benck's illness settled on the house like a pall. Amy tiptoed up and downstairs on mysterious messages; the green room door opened and shut. They did not like to go outside, and they could not settle to anything indoors. Twice they asked Amy in conscience-stricken tones: 'How is she?' and received the snappish reply: 'No better and no worse.'

The morning passed leadenly.

At last the specialist arrived from Edinburgh. He was a tall stout man with a head like an egg, broad at the chin and tapering into a narrow bald skull. He had ginger whiskers. He was most impressive. Doctor Narr was his name.

'Miss Sketheway?' he cried, pumping Auntie Robbo's hand. 'How d'you do? I'm very glad I've come in time. Is the patient upstairs? Yes, yes, in bed. Quiet's the thing, rest, rest, and quiet.'

'Show the doctor the way, Amy,' said Auntie Robbo. When they had disappeared upstairs, Auntie Robbo turned to Hector. 'He sounded quite different over the telephone,' she sighed. 'Quite charming. I never did like telephones. Still, perhaps he'll do her a lot of good. Like a nasty tonic.'

'M-m-m,' said Hector doubtfully.

They fidgeted about, waiting for the doctor to come down again. Half an hour passed.

'He *must* be doing her a lot of good,' said Auntie Robbo.

'She's terribly ill,' said Hector gloomily.

At last Auntie Robbo could stand the suspense no longer, and she was very hungry. She told Amy to go up and invite the doctor to join them at lunch. This brought him down almost immediately.

'Delightful of you,' he murmured, rubbing his pale plump hands, and sat down with them.

'How is Miss Benck?' Hector asked. 'Is she very ill?'

'That's a funny thing to call your stepmother, young man,' said the doctor jovially. Hector was taken aback. 'Isn't that her name?' he asked.

'Do tell us how she is,' interrupted Auntie Robbo. 'We've been very anxious about her.'

'Oh, there's nothing to worry about. Nothing at all. A slight chill. She's not used to our climate, you know. A few days quietly in bed and she'll be perfectly all right.'

Auntie Robbo and Hector sighed with relief, looking at each other; the feeling of guilt had rolled off them like a great stone.

Auntie Robbo's face wreathed itself in smiles. 'I *am* relieved,' she said. 'I'd really got into my head that the woman was going to die on us. Did you think so, Hector?'

Hector nodded.

'There you are. Such a fuss as there was in the house this

morning. Have some more soup, Doctor Narr? No? Then I will.'

'Miss Benck is very highly strung,' said the doctor.

'M-m-m. Hysterical type. I know them,' said Auntie Robbo judiciously. 'Had a cook once who used to take to her bed if a sauce was singed. Very pale she was. Just like Miss Benck. Anæmic.' Auntie Robbo was quite herself again, calm and confiding. Good nature bursting from her round brown face.

'No, no. Not hysterical. Sensitive is how I should describe Miss Benck. As her medical adviser, I assure you she's extremely sensitive. I don't think I've ever met such a sensitive woman.'

Auntie Robbo supped her soup noisily.

'She doesn't look hardy,' said Hector, trying to be polite. 'She's like a hothouse plant; overdone, you know. I expect Egypt is like a hothouse.'

Hector thought that a good speech, especially as Doctor Narr nodded gravely and sympathetically. But it was evidently too much for Auntie Robbo. She burst out laughing into her soup.

'Hector! Oh, Hector!' she spluttered. 'A hothouse plant! Oh, my goodness!' She got up from the table, convulsed with mirth. 'Excuse me, Doctor Narr, will you? I think I'll leave you to my nephew. He's quite entertaining, isn't he?' And she seized a chicken cutlet from the sideboard, clamped it between two rolls, and strode out of the room.

Doctor Narr had got to his feet in consternation; he seemed alarmed.

'It's quite all right,' said Hector mildly. 'Do sit down.'

Dr. Narr sat down. 'Does Miss Sketheway often behave like this?' he asked.

'On and off,' replied Hector.

'What do you mean, 'on and off'?' snapped the doctor 'How often?'

'When she feels like it.'

'Goodness gracious!' breathed Doctor Narr, his eyes of a sudden fixed on the dining-room window.

Auntie Robbo was standing on the white-painted summer seat outside. She had a long green cloak wrapped about her, and on her head a peaked green stalking cap, sitting very much askew. She leaned forward precariously, squidging her nose against the windowpane and contorting her mouth in expressive shouts.

Hector laughed, she looked so funny, and ran forward to open the window.

'Don't! Don't!' cried Doctor Narr. 'Don't let her in here!' He had backed round the table; his face had gone pale so that his gingery moustache looked like a wound, and he mopped at his brow with a napkin. 'It will pass in a minute. Dear boy, just let her alone. Let her calm down...'

But Hector had already opened the window. 'A little salt, please,' said Auntie Robbo.

Hector went to get a pinch of salt.

'Oh - and another roll. I'll away up to the Splash and give the wild ducks their dinner.' And when she had got her salt and her roll, Auntie Robbo called: 'Good-bye, Doctor Narr,'

lifted her little green cap with a flourish, bounded lightly off the summer seat, and passed out of sight.

Hector went back to his soup. Looking across at the doctor, he was surprised to find his gaze fixed earnestly and kindly upon him.

'Terrible! Terrible!' moaned Doctor Narr.

Hector furrowed his brows, looked doubtfully at the soup. It had seemed very good soup to him. 'Well, have some cutlets.' He rose and removed the doctor's plate. 'One or two?' asked Hector.

'Two,' said Doctor Narr morosely.

Hector set them before him and returned to his chair; he watched anxiously to see how the doctor liked his cutlets. But after a mouthful or two, Doctor Narr laid down his fork and again he gazed earnestly and sorrowfully at Hector, and again he murmured: 'Terrible! Terrible!'

'Young man!' He cleared his throat suddenly. 'I can see that you're very fond of your great-grand-aunt, but we must face the inevitable. The old tag *mens sana in corpore sano* doesn't hold good in all cases. By no means. Medical history is full of exceptions. We can see, for instance, that your great-grand-aunt is wonderfully healthy in her body, too healthy perhaps for a woman of her great years. Whence comes this wonderful strength? Is it not possible that if one part of this great engine which is our body functions overtime, another part may be running down, ever slower and slower, until it comes to a standstill? To keep the metaphor, for want of oil - petrol - steam - fuel - that's it, my dear boy, for want of fuel!'

Doctor Narr banged the table. Hector looked up for a moment. He had known as soon as he met Doctor Narr that he talked bilge, a different kind of bilge from Cousin Agnew or Merlissa Benck, but nevertheless bilge. He kept his ears politely closed against it. Now he saw that the conversation was still going nicely, although he hadn't taken in a word of it, and that Doctor Narr was enjoying himself. He returned to the business of eating chicken cutlets. The doctor's voice droned on:

'Yes, we must be prepared for such a thing happening - the slow deterioration of mental grasp in a loved one. And the more loved they are, the sooner we must face it, face it' - the doctor's voice rose - 'face it like men.' He leaned forward persuasively. 'Do you understand, my little man?'

Hector nodded, eating stolidly.

Doctor Narr gave a great sigh of relief. 'That's right. I didn't think you'd be so sensible.'

Then, with the pudding, he became expansive. 'To tell you the truth, young man, before I'd really seen your aunt, I was inclined to be a little sceptical of Merlissa Benck's story.' Hector opened his ears a fraction of an inch.

'You know, these nervous, highly-strung women are inclined to get ideas into their heads. However, your parlourmaid corroborated all she said, and of course I had only to be three minutes in Miss Sketheway's company to see exactly how the land lay. I've had too many cases like this to make a mistake.'

Hector stared at him with widening eyes.

'Poor little chap! You must have had a hard time of it all these years. However, all's well now. We'll get you packed off to school and you'll soon forget your little worries there.'

Doctor Narr laughed jovially, and came round the table to pat Hector on the head. Hector's scalp crept beneath his touch, but he remained docile and still, waiting intently for what Doctor Narr might say next.

'I think I'll step upstairs and put Miss Benck's mind at ease. And then I must rush back to town. There's so much to be done. I'll see Mrs. Agnew this afternoon. I think we'll be able to arrange about a suitable home for your great-grand-aunt. Don't worry, little man, she'll be in my care. I'll be back tomorrow, possibly with my colleague, Mr. Thurston; he's the great mind man, you know. Yes, well, good-bye, old chap. Don't worry.'

The door closed on him, and Hector was left alone. He sat quite still, listening to the doctor going upstairs, going into the green spare room, coming out, coming down again. He heard the front door bang, a car engine start up, and the gravel spurting against its wheels as it reversed on the drive. Then, as the sound of it died away, he suddenly leaped to his feet and tore out of the house to find Auntie Robbo.

CHAPTER SEVEN

The last hundred yards up the heather-clad slope which led to the Splash were almost too much for Hector. His legs were like to give under him, and his breath came in long strangled gasps, but excitement and fear kept him going. He knew that ordinarily he could never have run so far and so hard. As soon as he saw the tall, green-clad figure of Auntie Robbo, standing straight and motionless on the edge of the lochan, he tried to shout. The wind carried the sound ahead, and Auntie Robbo turned and waved. He stumbled over the last stretch of rough ground, and flung himself down at her feet; his whole body shook and throbbed against the turf.

'I've had the drake right in,' said Auntie Robbo triumphantly. 'Almost feeding out of my hand! I stood so still I might have been a tree for all he knew. It's wet there, Hector. Come and

sit over here on this slab of stone.'

Auntie Robbo went over to pull him, then saw what a state he was in. 'You must have been running hard!' she said.

Hector looked wildly at her but could not say a word. She helped him to his feet and together they sat down on the stone, with the green cloak spread amply beneath them.

Something of his anxiety communicated itself to Auntie Robbo. 'What is it, Hector? What's the matter?'

'Doctor,' gasped Hector. 'Mad!'

Auntie Robbo laughed. 'What has he been doing? Has he

given the wrong dose to Merlissa Benck - or did he go for Amy with an axe? He struck me as being a little quaint, but not mad, not mad.'

'They're all mad,' cried Hector, 'all mad down there!' His breath was coming more easily now; he looked with horror down at the smoking chimney-pots of Nethermuir. 'But it's not that I came to tell you, not exactly that. *He* thinks *you're* mad.'

Auntie Robbo was pleasantly amused. 'Oh, because of the way I went out. He's not very original in his conclusions. An aunt of mine was the first person to think that - Aunt Sibella, about seventy years ago, that was - and people have been thinking it on and off ever since. *I* don't mind, and it seems to give them some sort of relief. Do tell me what he said, Hector.'

Hector did so, everything that he could remember. In his despair of making her understand how serious a matter it was, not funny at all, he repeated things over and over again - how plain the plot was to get him adopted by Merlissa Benck, how horrible the doctor was, how Amy had helped, what a sure way it was of getting Auntie Robbo out of the way for ever and ever. Auntie Robbo asked him a question or two at the end, and then sat still, gazing at the ducks on the far side of the Splash. Her face was grave and a little sad, an expression that Hector had scarcely ever seen on it. She passed her hand over her forehead, and said in a small, rather pathetic voice. 'Perhaps he's right! Perhaps I am a little mad.'

Hector leaped to his feet, grinning: 'Stop play-acting,

Auntie Robbo. Do be serious.'

Auntie Robbo grinned too. 'Imagine, at my time of life. I thought I'd got over the necessity for play-acting a long time ago. Still, it is disconcerting to find what other people think of one. One can't help feeling for a moment that there might be some truth in it - for a moment.'

'Not even for a moment!' cried Hector. 'Who could believe a word that Merlissa Benck says? And as for that tappy a doctor - of course he's a tappy. Look at the shape of his head.'

She laughed.

'But what are we to do?' asked Hector, fear and anxiety flooding his mind again.

'Do? I don't know that we can do anything very much until the time comes. Then we'll just turn the tables on them, and send Merlissa Benck packing in the doctor's car. I hope Cousin Agnew comes. That will be fun.'

Hector's brow had not cleared.

'Goodness, Hector, you don't think they can clap me into a padded cell without some sort of a formality. They'll have to give me a proper examination, ask me questions, make me walk along a white line - that sort of thing. I shall do it frightfully well, I promise you. Unless I laugh. If Cousin Agnew is there, I expect I shall laugh.'

'But you don't understand, Auntie Robbo. Please, please listen. They're all wicked, they're evil, they're crooks, they won't stop at anything - '

'Hector, you've been reading Amy's thrillers. Nobody is like that. They're just stupid.'

'They're greedy as well. They're stupid and greedy, and that's the same thing in the long run - '

Auntie Robbo smiled, nodding. 'Yes, isn't it strange?' She remained thoughtful for a moment or two, and then suggested lightly: 'Well, we could go away, you know. We needn't wait for the white line and Cousin Agnew's long face. Would that be better?'

'Could we?' breathed Hector. 'When?'

She lowered her voice in a thrilling whisper. 'As soon as it's dark. Bus at the end of the road. About seven. I always see it when I'm dressing.'

Hector jumped up in his excitement; this was much better; this was right; this was what you expected from Auntie Robbo!

Now they began to talk eagerly over their escape and the discomfiture of Merlissa Benck. They thought they would go north to the Highlands, for that was the proper place to go for an escape. They hoped Merlissa Benck would go back to Egypt - or marry Doctor Narr. A good hour passed by up at the Splash. Hector played ducks and drakes with the fine flat stones on the shore; Auntie Robbo paced up and down, pausing to make some suggestion from time to time. When they came down the hill together they were in great good spirits.

Passing the stables on their way into the house, Hector was struck by a sudden idea.

'Merlissa Benck's car!' he said. 'We ought to do something about it. She could follow the bus in it tonight.'

'What do you mean? Smash it up?'

They went into the harness room where the car was temporarily garaged. 'It would be a big job,' said Auntie Robbo dubiously.

'No, you just take something out of the works - a little thing, a cog or a nut or something. I've read about it. Then it can't go.'

'Where *are* the works?' She opened one of the doors and peered inside.

'They're in front,' explained Hector, and while he struggled to raise the bonnet, Auntie Robbo picked up a hammer.

There were a great many screws and bolts inside the bonnet, so they fiddled at some of them, and the rest Auntie Robbo banged with her hammer.

Presently Hector said he thought they had done enough; he looked rather ruefully at the mess they had made inside the shining blue car; he felt as if he had committed a murder. But Auntie Robbo just said: 'Never did like machines. Ever since I got sewed into a sheet my mother was hemming on one.' She went on striking vigorously, denting the bonnet and mudguards.

'That's enough now. Do stop,' Hector cried. 'Amy will be out to see what's happening!'

Auntie Robbo laid the hammer down reluctantly. They washed their hands under the yard tap, and went into the house.

Hearing them laughing and talking in the hall, Amy came out of the kitchen. 'Miss Benck is a little easier, ma'am.' she glared at Hector, who was whistling blithely. 'But she's still far from well.'

Hector stopped whistling. He and Auntie Robbo turned and looked at her broodingly. There was something so peculiar in their look, not at all cowed or rebuked, that Amy turned uneasily on her way upstairs. She wished she had not said anything then. After all, it was only till tomorrow...

Auntie Robbo and Hector went upstairs after her to do their packing.

'Now remember,' whispered Auntie Robbo, 'we don't want much baggage. Only bare necessities.'

So Auntie Robbo went to her room and pulled out a big old-fashioned wicker case from her wardrobe and put into it a yachting costume, a shooting costume, her purple dress with the diamond tassels, a pot of balsam to keep the midges off, all her jewels, of which she was very fond, a tartan plaid, three changes of underwear, a pair of binoculars, and a sketch book and paints. Not that Auntie Robbo liked sketching or *could* sketch, but she vaguely remembered that the last time she had been in the Highlands, while the gentlemen shot, the ladies of the party had been expected to make pictures of the mountain and river scenery. It was the proper thing to do while visiting the Highlands. Auntie Robbo had gone off to look for cloudberries instead with a handsome gillie. Still, she thought this time she might try the sketching. As a lucky afterthought she tossed a cheque-book and some bank notes into the case and jammed it shut.

Meanwhile Hector had got out a little Gladstone bag, and

even when he had put his pyjamas and his toothbrush into it, it still seemed very empty. So he added, though somewhat against his conscience, one clean shirt.

By the time the dressing gong had gone, they were each, in their separate rooms, sitting ready in their outdoor things with their bags beside them. They listened till the note of the gong had died away and Amy's footsteps had receded to the kitchen. Then they stole out, meeting on the landing. Auntie Robbo made a face in the direction of Merlissa Benck's room. They crept down the stairs, opened the front door cautiously, and were out into the night.

The gravel made a horrid crunching noise under their feet, but at last they gained the grass verge and hurried away down the drive. By the time they reached the gate, Auntie Robbo was panting and grunting under the weight of her bulging case. Hector took one of the handles with her.

Everything had gone according to schedule, and they had hardly stood a minute or two by the side of the main road when they heard the roar of engines, and the great bus with its double row of lighted windows and staring sign EDINBURGH came bearing down on them. Auntie Robbo stepped out bravely before the headlights of the monster, waving her handkerchief. Right to the last minute Hector had been afraid something would go wrong, and he heaved a sigh of thankfulness when the bus drew to a standstill for them. He and Auntie Robbo jumped in.

Up at Nethermuir, Amy paused in laying the dining-room table and wondered why the bus was stopping. For quite half an hour afterwards she expected a visitor - the minister or the cook's young man. But no one came.

CHAPTER EIGHT

As the bus sped forwards into the dark and drumly night, Auntie Robbo's and Hector's spirits bounced higher with every bounce of their bodies on the bumpy top-front seat. They congratulated themselves on the coolness and cleverness of their escape. They marvelled at their mode of conveyance - perched so high that sometimes tree branches hit the roof, and far below the road swam and swayed as if it had been a river at the bottom of a canyon. They had never been on a bus at night before. Auntie Robbo said it was an improvement on being in a bus by day. They bounced and beamed each other in great contentment over the twelve miles to Edinburgh.

When the bus reached the city and they travelled down the yellow-lighted bustling streets, Hector got so excited he had to cheer. He wanted all the people hurrying back and forth, or standing talking in doorways, to look up and wave to him and Auntie Robbo, to congratulate them on their marvellous escape. But the crowds were all intent upon their own business and I dare say would have thought that there was nothing much in travelling twelve miles through the night in a double-decker bus. Auntie Robbo and Hector kept pointing out things to each other, a strange name over a shop, a greyhound led on a string, a fat policeman running.

They got off the bus opposite the General Post-Office.

'Now I've all sorts of schemes,' said Auntie Robbo. 'First a telegram to Nethermuir - '

'But - ' began Hector.

'I know they'll get it in no time, but not before we're in our train to Perth. Besides I shall put them off the scent. I'll pretend we've gone to London. We must let them know something. Otherwise these two fool women will have the countryside in an uproar, looking for us. They'll be dragging the Splash tomorrow, like as not, and frightening the wild duck away.'

By this time they were across the street and entering the Post-Office. 'You look after the baggage,' said Auntie Robbo.

Hector sat down beside their cases at one of the big tables that ran down the centre of the room. He looked round him; he had never been there before. It was a great imposing place with ugly red tiles on the floor and imitation marble pillars and a counter running the whole length of it, surmounted by an iron grid; behind the grid bobbed little men, stamping and writing and working with money and looking very important. The Post-Office was full of people; every second its swing door swung, letting out some of them or letting in some more; there was a continual draught and many collisions; people streamed to and from the counter, rain-soaked, hurrying, all bent on posting big parcels or important letters or sending telegrams or using the row of telephone booths; the little men behind the counter bobbed frantically. Hector was impressed; nobody seemed to be still, doing nothing, except himself. And then he noticed the people at the next table. They were three children, two boys and a girl, and they were bent over a sheet of paper. At first he thought they must be sending a telegram or writing a letter just like anybody else; but every now and then they straightened up and laughed into each other's faces. And then they looked across at one of the Post-Office men behind the grid and laughed some more. Hector edged along nearer and saw that the boy in the middle was busy drawing on the back of a telegram form. The girl leaned on his left shoulder, breathing heavily, with interest; she was rather like the boy who was drawing. They both had peaked bony faces, bright black eyes, and a deal of black hair that grew long and lank, dangling forward into their eyes. The girl wore an old black tammy on the back of her head. She kept moving her feet as if they were cold in a floppity, down-at-heel pair of shoes. The other boy was round-faced and red-haired; he had on long trousers that seemed to be much too big in the seat for him. He kept them hitched up in position with his hands in his pockets;

and every now and then he would take a few steps backwards on his heels, bent double, and then run forward again to see how the drawing was getting on. Hector was dying to have a look: he edged a bit nearer still but just as he was craning his neck to see, the man from behind the grid - the one the children had been looking at - was suddenly, miraculously, no longer behind the grid but there before them at their table.

'Out you go, the lot of you!' he said to the three children.

'You've no business here. I've had my eye on you this last half-hour.'

'Aw, mister,' said the girl pouting.

The boy who had been drawing chimed in: 'It's raining and we haven't any place to go.'

'I can't help that,' said the man. 'This is a post-office, not a playground. Now then, get along with you.'

The red-haired boy perked up with a smile. 'If we had another tanner we could go to the pictures.'

The man fixed them with an awful eye. He spoke as if he could hardly believe his ears. 'Begging!' he said. 'Begging in a Government building! Do I have to get a policeman to you or will you go quiet?'

The children backed away from him to the nearest swing door, and whisked themselves out into the night.

They had left their telegram form on the table. The man looked at it an instant, then angrily crumpled it up and flung it into a wastepaper basket. No sooner was his back turned than Hector had fished it out again. He smoothed it; on it was an easily recognizable portrait of the Post-Office man, only he had been changed into a monkey clinging to the bars of his grid and a passer-by was handing him a bun.

'What are you laughing at?' asked Auntie Robbo, coming back. 'Never mind now. Tell me in the train. We've got things to do.'

She hurried him out of the Post-Office, across the street, and up the steps of a big hotel.

'Mind the bags, Hector,' said Auntie Robbo again. And when she had talked a minute at the desk in the entrance hall, presently a man came with black tails flying and starched shirt front gleaming. He bowed before Auntie Robbo and waited with notebook outstretched, and poised pencil.

'A big basket,' said Auntie Robbo, 'for it's a celebration supper. And it must have cold roast chicken in it, potato straws, rolls and salad, a bottle of claret bring me the wine list - and milk for my nephew, biscuits and cheese...' Auntie Robbo paused. 'Yes, Stilton, too, meringues and a jar of cream, two fresh peaches, and a box of chocolates.'

'Is that all, madam?'

'Yes, that's all, I think. Now I give you just ten minutes to get that ready, young man, in time for my train.'

The waiter fled. Auntie Robbo said: 'We're going to eat all the way from here to Perth, Hector.'

'D'you think we'll be able for all that?' he asked.

'Eh?' said Auntie Robbo anxiously. 'I'm very hungry myself. Perhaps I let my appetite get the better of me.'

Hector reached down through the lair of his excitement to consider his stomach, and found to his surprise that it was indeed very empty.

Auntie Robbo was relieved to hear it. They paced up and down for a few minutes and then sat down on a couch while Hector told Auntie Robbo of the three children he had seen being turned out of the Post-Office. When he showed her the picture Auntie Robbo was impressed, for she recognized the monkey at once. 'He was next to the one who took my telegram. I remember because I thought myself if I'd had a bun I would have been tempted to push it through the bars.' She laughed heartily.

Just then the waiter returned carrying a wicker basket. Auntie Robbo congratulated him on being in time, and gave him a lot of money. She waved away a man who was going to pick up their bags, and she and Hector between them loaded up and struggled down lots of stairs and along lots of corridors, all carpeted deeply and hung with curtains. And lo! when they had pushed through the last swing door, the luxurious hotel had given place to a great dirty station. 'Tickets first!' puffed Auntie Robbo. She got them at the booking-office, and then returned to Hector. 'The train leaves from that platform over there. It isn't in yet. May as well sit down for a few minutes.'

She indicated a door marked 'General Waiting-Room,' and they went inside.

Hector noticed three children immediately; they were the same three who had been in the Post-Office. There they were grouped together at the far end of the room, laughing at what the black-haired boy was drawing on a piece of paper.

Hector nudged Auntie Robbo urgently. 'It's them!' he whispered. The eyes of the three children were fixed on the only other people in the waiting-room - an elderly gaunt-faced woman neatly dressed in navy-blue, with three small boys in her charge. These boys seemed to be all about the same age and height. They had round button faces and turned-up noses; they wore spectacles upon their turned-up noses which gave them a comic elderly look; they had little round felt hats turned up all round the brim.

At the far end of the room the picture seemed to be going well; the girl and the red-haired boy giggled at every stroke of their artist's pencil, and he - when it was a particularly happy one - would let out a sharp whistle of triumph. But his models were becoming more and more restless and embarrassed. At last the elderly woman could bear it no longer. 'Let us go to the Ladies' First-Class Waiting-Room,' she said stiffly, rising. 'It will be quieter.'

'Will *they* come, Miss Comrie?' asked one of the bespectacled small boys. 'Of course not. Pay no attention,' she whispered.

'I think they're very rude.'

'Yes, very rude. Come along now. We mustn't miss your uncle.'

She shepherded her charges out. The three children sent a shout of laughter after her disgruntled back. Then with one accord they turned and stared at Auntie Robbo and Hector. The black-haired boy licked his pencil.

'Our turn now,' whispered Auntie Robbo grinning. She

put her hat on straight.

The boy who drew turned his paper over thoughtfully and made a few lines. The other two watched absorbed.

Then just as they raised their eyes again to Auntie Robbo and Hector, the waiting-room door swung open and in rushed a funny little man in a flapping tweed overcoat. He was young, yet he looked careworn and flustered enough to be middle-aged. On the top of his head he wore a round pimply tweed hat, turned up all along the brim. His face was button-shaped and he had a snub nose.

'Oh, there you are!' he shouted, making straight for the three children in the corner. 'I've been hunting for you up and down this station.'

The children looked frightened, and backed away from him round the table. 'Where's Miss Comrie?' he cried. 'Why isn't she here?'

The girl piped up: 'Please, sir, she went to the Ladies' Waiting-Room.'

'Well, come along, come along. We can't wait about for her, the train's just going. Hurry up now. Platform ten. Run for it,' and he shooed them out before him through the door.

Auntie Robbo and Hector looked at each other, not knowing what to make of the incident, then Auntie Robbo leapt up, scrambling for their bags. 'Hurry, Hector. Platform ten, that's ours.'

They staggered out of the waiting-room and across the station in the wake of the man and the three children. They showed their tickets and followed them through the gate.

They ran with them the length of the train, looking for a carriage that wasn't too full. And in despair they bundled into the same one as the man and the children did, just as the guard began to bang all the doors. In a few seconds the train was steaming out of the station.

CHAPTER NINE

'Well, that was a near thing!' said Auntie Robbo to the carriage at large.

They had got their things hoisted into the rack with a deal of bumping and apologizing, and now they had all settled back in their seats, breathing heavily. Auntie Robbo mopped her brow with a six-inch square of lace handkerchief. She and Hector sat facing the young-old man and the three children. And though they sat so demurely, looking out as the lighted buildings and streets of Edinburgh whirled away behind them, Hector could see that the children were consumed with mirth inside themselves. Every now and then they nudged each other or burst out coughing.

As for the young-old man he was too busy putting away the tickets and panting for breath to notice anything. But he replied to Auntie Robbo: 'Very close, very close, madam. There's nothing more upsetting than catching a train by the skin of one's teeth. I'd much sooner miss it. Really. My nerves. Can't stand it.'

He put away his pocket-book, patting it into place. 'Now there's sure to be something left behind. There always is. Let me see. Got the tickets, got the children ... oh, dear me, the luggage! That was to go straight through from London. But you never can trust these railway people. I wonder if it's in the guard's van. I wonder if Miss Comrie looked. She's supposed to be a good sensible woman. Surely ... did Miss Comrie see that the luggage was all right?' he asked, turning to the red-haired boy at his side.

The boy looked blank, then shook his head.

'Bless me, I shall have to go at once and see about it. Oh, what a silly woman! I might have known something would go wrong.'

He got up. 'Would you be so kind as to keep an eye on my three nephews?' he said to Auntie Robbo. 'I'm sure they'll all be good quiet boys.' He turned, wagging an admonitory forefinger at the three children. They giggled hysterically. Auntie Robbo opened her eyes and said innocently: 'But they aren't.'

'What? What? Aren't good? I should like to know...'

'Aren't boys,' explained Auntie Robbo and began to laugh.

The children began to laugh out loud. The young-old man looked around in bewilderment.

'I mean,' gasped Auntie Robbo, 'not three boys. You left

them with Miss Comrie. These are two boys and a girl.'

The young-old man was utterly flabbergasted; his mouth hung open, his eyes bulged, and as he hunted desperately through some inner pockets, he stuttered: 'What do you mean? I say - what's all this? A girl among my nephews! Couldn't possibly - what do you mean?'

At last he succeeded in finding a spectacle case, and from it he produced and perched on his nose a thick-lensed pair of horn-rimmed glasses.

He took one look at the children and collapsed back into his seat. For a second everybody thought he had fainted. But suddenly he leaped up in the lurching car, shouting: 'These aren't mine! They're impostors! Impostors! Gutter-snipes! There's been a conspiracy. I'll have the law on you. I'll stop the train.' He clutched wildly upwards for the communication cord, but since his glasses slipped off sideways he missed it by about a foot.

After finding and adjusting the glasses, he again reached upwards; the rest of the carriage was tense with excitement. The three strange children were pressed back against their seats, open-mouthed, as if a madman with a bomb were in their midst. Hector had his hands over his eyes and looked through his fingers at the unbearably thrilling scene. Only Auntie Robbo remained comparatively calm, leaning forward a little, tapping her front teeth thoughtfully, as if she had been at an interesting play.

His fingers touched the fateful chain, and then, whether the train lurched again or he caught sight of the fateful notice, his hand faltered. It said there was five pounds' fine for stopping the train, except in emergency.

'Go on,' breathed the girl in the corner. She spoke for them all.

'Yes, do,' said Auntie Robbo encouragingly. 'What's five pounds? It's worth it, man, every penny.'

The young-old man subsided abruptly into his seat.

Everybody looked reproachfully at him: and at the same time the air in the compartment became definitely less difficult to breathe, lighter and easier on the lungs. Just as they were going to say how much they had wanted to see the communication cord pulled, the young-old man suddenly took out a handkerchief and burst into tears. The atmosphere immediately became surcharged again. All the children were wide-eyed with interest; for a moment they couldn't imagine what was wrong with him, such queer noises came out of the handkerchief.

'Come, come,' said Auntie Robbo, patting him on the knee.

The young man continued to wheeze and wail with complete abandon.

'Get down the basket, Hector,' shouted Auntie Robbo; and shortly she had pulled the cork from her bottle of claret and poured out a glassful.

'Here you are, young-old man,' she cried, shoving the glass between his face and his handkerchief. 'This'll do you good.'

The young-old man stared at her, with the tears rolling down his cheek. 'Never touch spirits,' he hissed.

'It isn't spirits. It's wine. It's just what you need.'

The young-old man sipped obediently. 'My nerves,' he said. 'I suffer terribly from my nerves.'

'We can see that,' said Auntie Robbo soothingly. 'And of course it has been a great surprise to you. We have all been greatly surprised, haven't we?'

'Yes,' said Hector, and the other children. 'That's right,' added the red-haired boy.

Everybody waited expectantly while the young-old man finished his glass of claret. 'But what happened?' he wailed at last. 'What am I to do?'

Auntie Robbo hastened to explain, in case he should start crying again. 'You see, we were all sitting in the general waiting-room, just waiting...' and she told him about Miss Comrie and his three nephews, and how they had gone away, and then he himself had come sweeping in and rushed them all off to the train before they quite knew where they were. 'You ought to wear your spectacles if you're as short-sighted as all that.'

'Yes, but I keep losing them if I wear them,' said the young-old man pathetically. 'Oh, dear, I knew something would go wrong. You see my brother and sister-in-law have gone abroad and their three boys were to come to us for the holidays. Miss Comrie is their governess - she wasn't coming - she was going to Troon for her holidays. I don't know what my mother will say when I turn up without them. She hasn't seen them since they were babies and she'll be terribly disappointed. And when she's disappointed, she gets terribly angry. Oh, dear, oh, dear, what a mess I've made of things.'

'Yes, you have, I should think,' said Auntie Robbo. 'And what you're going to do with these three children you've picked up, I should very much like to know.'

The young-old man gave a little yelp. 'Aren't they yours?'

'Oh, no,' said Auntie Robbo. 'Only this one is mine. This is my great-grand-nephew, Hector Murdoch.'

Hector got up and shook hands politely.

'Oh, really ... oh,' gasped the young-old man. 'My name is Burston, Brinsley Burston. And who are you?' He got up, shouting violently at the three strange children. 'I don't care who or what you are! You're nothing to do with me. Out you get at the first stop and I'll hand you over to the police.'

'Your nerves,' cried Auntie Robbo. 'What about your nerves!' She and Hector pulled him by the coat-tails until he had to sit down again.

'Yes, who are you now?' asked Auntie Robbo. 'And tell us your side of the story.'

The children wriggled shyly a moment. And then the girl, putting on a laconic air, jerked her thumb at the red-haired boy: 'That's Sando, my brother. He's got a job as a baker's boy. And this is Pete. He's our cousin. He wants to be an artist. And I'm Mary.'

She smiled disarmingly and waited.

'Yes, but where do you come from, where do you live?' cried the young-old man.

'Well, sometimes we live with our stepfather - Sando's and mine. Pete comes too. And other times we live with Pete's aunt. It just depends.'

'Depends on what?' Auntie Robbo asked. 'On *them*,' explained Pete.

'Oh.'

The group digested all this information in silence. And then the young-old man broke out again. 'That doesn't matter. What I want to know is what you're doing here? Now - out with it!'

Auntie Robbo sighed. 'You'd better tell him,' she said.

'*He* took us,' said Mary, pointing indignantly at the young-old man.

'That's right,' agreed the red-haired boy. 'We were sitting peaceable-like in the waiting-room, just waiting, like you were saying, and Pete was doing a bit of drawing just to pass the time, and *he* came in and told us to come on. So we came on. We thought he was the police. But it's kidnapping, if you ask me.'

'Well, there you are, Mr. Burston,' said Auntie Robbo. 'And I must say that's just the way I thought it happened. I'd bear witness to that in any court in the land.'

Mr. Burston looked as if he was going to cry again. 'Why didn't you say something? Why weren't you home in bed? Why weren't your beastly aunts and stepfathers there to look after you? It's a scandal, children left lying about loose in railway stations. It would have served you right if I had kidnapped you.'

'Och, we wouldna have cared,' said the red-haired boy.

'No, why should we?' chimed in Mary. 'We're not doing

anything.'

'What about Pete's aunt and your stepfather?' Auntie Robbo asked.

'Oh, *them*,' said Pete. He hardly ever opened his mouth, but when he did it was most expressively.

'They don't bother much,' Sando explained. 'Except when they're foo. They'll never miss us for a day or two.'

'A day or two?' Brinsley Burston's voice rose quaveringly.

'It's quite obvious that you'll have to do something about them, Mr. Burston,' said Auntie Robbo. 'But I'm too hungry at the moment to discuss it. Let's all have something to eat.'

She opened the sumptuous hotel basket. 'There ought to be a bite to go round,' she said. Mary and Sando and Pete and Hector sat up expectantly.

Brinsley Burston snapped his fingers. 'Food!' he groaned, looking out of the window.

But when Auntie Robbo handed him a cardboard plate full of chicken and potato and salad, he took it unresistingly and was soon absorbed, with a handkerchief tucked under his chin, a roll on one knee, and a wineglass at his elbow, making a hearty meal.

As for the others, they shared the rest of the chicken between them and finished up every scrap of the things that went with it. Auntie Robbo drank out of the claret bottle, much to Sando's admiration. He said he had never seen any other woman able to do that without spluttering, even Pete's aunt, who was by way of being a hardened, life-long drinker.

'It only needs intelligence,' said Auntie Robbo. 'Intelligence and practice.'

The children practised with the milk bottle. Some milk unfortunately got spilt on Brinsley Burston's coat. Auntie Robbo quickly gave him a peach before he should notice it. The children ate meringues, licking the cream up like cats.

'I'm beginning to feel a little better,' sighed Brinsley Burston when he had finished his peach.

'I'm sure you do,' agreed Auntie Robbo. 'Now we can decide what is best to be done.'

'I feel fine,' cried Sando, beating his stomach. 'Better than fish and chips.'

They packed the debris back into the basket, and then they lay back dreamifly munching chocolates.

Perhaps, of them all, only Hector was giving more thought to the problem before them than to his stomach. He spoke at last: 'Mr. Burston, didn't you say that your mother didn't really know what your nephews looked like?'

'Yes, did I? She's very fond of them for all that. They live in the south of England, you know.'

'Well, if she's never seen them, you can just say these are them,' said Hector triumphantly. 'And then she'll be pleased, and you'll be pleased, and Pete and Mary and Sando will be pleased. Everything will be all right.'

'How clever of you, Hector!' said Auntie Robbo. 'Don't you think that's a good idea, Mr. Burston?'

Brinsley Burston struggled against her honeyed tones. 'Certainly not,' he tried to say indignantly, and then ended in a weak voice: 'Anyway, they aren't three boys. My mother would detect the difference at once.'

Auntie Robbo was not in the least put out. 'You could borrow Hector,' she said, 'and I could have the girl instead. Let me see, where do you live?'

'Just outside Stirling.'

'Splendid. That will do us very nicely. We were going to Perth but it doesn't really matter. I will be Miss Comrie; at the last moment I sacrificed my holiday in order to come and keep an eye on the boys. Mary will be my niece. I had to bring her because I promised to take her to Troon. Would you like to be my niece, Mary?'

Mary nodded, speechless with enthusiasm.

'Well, there you are,' said Auntie Robbo, with an easy gesture of her hands. 'All settled, Mr. Burston. A load off your mind, I'm sure. Now don't fret yourself about where we're going to sleep or anything like that--we don't mind in the least. An attic will do me. But what is your cook like? That's really important.'

'It's not that, Miss... Mrs...'

'Call me Miss Comrie, then you'll get used to it.'

'It isn't that at all. It's the deception. I can't be a party to....'

'Oh, dear, the deception!' cried Auntie Robbo, and bit the tips of her fingers. 'I quite forgot. You'll have to stop the real Miss Comrie from turning up with your three nephews, or from making inquiries. I'll tell you what: send them a telegram to their hotel; say there's an epidemic raging in the neighbourhood and that they'd much better not come till next year. I expect the governess will take them straight back home, all the better and none the wiser for their little trip to Edinburgh. Or she may take them to Troon. Troon's very nice, I believe. Have another chocolate? That's a marzipan and that one there's a strawberry liqueur, judging by the mess on Sando's face.'

Brinsley Burston looked disgustedly at Sando. 'Which is the marzipan?' he asked, and when he had picked it and eaten it his brow seemed to have cleared.

'You really think this is the best thing to do - under the circumstances?' he said at length.

'Well, not perhaps the best,' Auntie Robbo replied, 'but I think it's a very good thing. I mean we're all friends by this time, and I think it would be a pity just to dump Sando and Pete and Mary or send them back to the aunt-stepfather combination. Then we don't want to disappoint your mother, do we?'

'That's right,' agreed Sando.

Auntie Robbo looked at him affectionately and handed him the box of chocolates.

Everyone waited to see if Mr. Burston would say anything; but the train rattled on through the darkness, the light blinkered in the roof of the coach, the rain-drops sped down the windowpanes, and still Brinsley Burston only looked out at his own reflection and sighed occasionally. Pete drew a picture of him, breathing on the glass. He looked at it and only sighed the more. So they concluded that his silence could only mean consent to the scheme.

CHAPTER TEN

Making a fine plan is all very well, especially when you are sitting back in a railway coach, flying through the night, feeling full of food and sleepy and irresponsible. But when you have to carry out that plan, it is a very different matter.

In the next seven hectic days, Hector often wished that he had never suggested that Brinsley Burston should do anything so silly as to take home three false nephews; and he wished oftener that Auntie Robbo hadn't had the diabolical idea of making him one of them and herself the governess. Not that the plan was unsuccessful; Auntie Robbo saw to that; but it was its very success that made it trying in the long run.

They did not see Mrs. Burston on the night of their arrival. It was late and she had gone to bed. 'She's not at all strong,' explained Brinsley, and he winced as if his conscience had given him a sudden jab.

So Auntie Robbo had time to groom Sando and Pete both in their parts and persons. Haircuts. Baths. Clothes.

The trunks of the real little Burstons *had* been put safely in the luggage-van; the children all stood in an excited circle while Auntie Robbo picked the locks with a hairpin.

'It's not so easy as it looks,' she said, 'but I've had lots of practice. Now stand back till we see what you can wear.'

She began to rummage among the clothes, tossing garments to Pete and Sando and Hector - velveteen knickerbockers, silk blouses, combinations, white jerseys, buckled shoes, panama hats. Their faces lengthened.

'Try some on,' she commanded.

'Can't I wear my own trousers?' pleaded Sando. They had belonged to the baker who had employed him, and he was very fond of them.

Auntie Robbo shook her head. 'Not at first, at any rate.'

The boys struggled into some of the things. Mary giggled.

'I've got a clean shirt in my bag,' protested Hector. 'Surely that's enough?'

'They're sissy, that's what they are,' said Sando gloomily.

Pete said nothing, standing in a pair of pink one-piece pyjamas which buttoned down the front and reached only to his knees. He wore a little pimply black hat perched on top of his head. He grinned.

'They don't seem quite right,' said Auntie Robbo, frowning: 'What d'you think, Mary?'

'They're too small,' said Mary.

'Oh, well, never mind, they'll do for a start. I'll get you some more in the town tomorrow.'

At that moment Brinsley Burston popped his head round the door, saying he had just remembered about the way Sando and Pete and Hector talked; they shouldn't have a Scots accent. He looked most unhappy.

'Oh, all right!' said Auntie Robbo, and he disappeared.

But Sando flatly refused to 'talk proper', and Hector said the way he talked was the way he talked and how could anybody change the way he talked? Pete said nothing.

'Well, do your best,' pleaded Auntie Robbo. 'It'll only be for a day or two. After that it will be all right; she'll just think you've picked up the accent here.'

Then they all went wearily and rather huffily to bed; all except Mary, who was enjoying being Auntie Robbo's niece.

The next morning they met Mrs. Burston at breakfast. She turned out to be only an older and more feminine Brinsley, even to her extreme shortsightedness (which was lucky) and her nervous ailments, which were so numerous that she rarely stirred from her armchair. She was a little soft-looking old lady with fleecy white hair and a lot of fleecy white shawls. Her voice was fretful and bleating like a sheep that has got on the wrong side of a dyke. She made a great deal of fuss about 'draughts' and 'absolute quiet' and 'my bad days'. But she was a very gentle, sweet-looking old lady for all that.

She was delighted when her three grandsons were presented to her - Alexander, Peter, and Hector. (Actually the real little Burstons were called Simon, Peter, and James, but Auntie Robbo said she was sure Mrs. Burston would never notice. Nor did she.) She immediately traced Sando's red hair back to her own father, thought that Pete must be like his mother's side of the family, and as for Hector - he was the living image of what his Uncle Brinsley had been at that age. Sando and Pete seemed quite pleased with the situation, grinning and saying in affected voices that they were quite well thank you and hoped she was the same. But Hector didn't relish the business at all; he squirmed and grew red and wouldn't say a word.

Old Mrs. Burston seemed to be relieved by Auntie Robbo's presence. 'The boys are a little bigger than I expected, Miss Comrie,' she sighed. 'It will be nice to have you here to manage them.'

It was harder to get her to accept Mary as a natural event, but Brinsley achieved it in the end by showing how useful she would be about the house, making beds and mending socks, and so on, while Auntie Robbo was coping with the boys.

'They're very high-spirited boys then?' asked Mrs. Burston.

'Oh, very,' Auntie Robbo assured her.

'Well, I suppose it's a good thing,' quavered Mrs. Burston. 'You were a very low-spirited little boy, Brinsley. I suppose it will be nice to have a change.'

And so they were accepted into the household that first morning.

The Burstons lived in a stolid Victorian villa just on the outskirts of Stirling; behind were stables with a loft and a big garden, and the children soon found it was best to spend most of their time there.

During the first few days Pete and Sando and Hector were absorbed in making each other's acquaintance. Hector had been a little unsure of them at first; they were older than he was, Sando by nearly four years, Pete by two; but they were not much bigger. Pete never said very much, nor gave away what he was thinking; and yet Hector began to feel that he was a very sensible sort of boy, almost as sensible as himself. Without being aware of it, they became fast friends. Pete did for Sando what Hector did for Auntie Robbo; he kept an eye on him. For Sando was a simple creature who always got himself into trouble; almost everything amused and pleased him; and anything that didn't please him he wanted to smash or fight. He liked Hector, fortunately.

But he didn't like the bed he had to sleep in; that caused the first row with Brinsley Burston. Sando bumped his head on one of the knobs as he got into it, and this annoyed him so much he sawed all the knobs off it, the next morning, and one or two off the rest of the furniture as well. Brinsley nearly had hysterics. 'Young hooligan!' he shrieked. 'Doesn't know how to behave in a civilized house.'

'Well, the knobs were no use,' Auntie Robbo tried to pacify him. 'I mean, don't you think the bed's quite as good without them? One can still sleep in it.'

'That's right,' said Sando, 'that's what I thought.'

They played lots of games in the garden, climbing about the trees and outhouses, chasing each other as cowboys and Indians, Scots and English, Fascists and Communists. But by and by the flower beds and vegetables began to assume such an air of havoc that Brinsley put a ban on these games. He went to Stirling and bought a set of clock golf for them. It was great fun setting it up; they dug a hole for the ball in the middle of the lawn as deep and wide almost as a grave. But somehow the game didn't catch on; not until Pete thought of

the brilliant idea of making a *real* golf course in the garden. It had all sorts of improbable hazards; for instance, the ball had to be played into the lily pond instead of over it; then out again, wading; then over the greenhouse, through the tool-shed window, in and out the gooseberry bushes, between the rows of vegetables, up onto the stable roof, and from there it was holed out on the lawn. They only played it once that way. Brinsley took the clubs away from them.

By the third day Brinsley was beginning to wear that anxious, distraught look they had first found him with in the train.

Meanwhile Auntie Robbo was getting along nicely in her different sphere 'below stairs'. Mary had become very attached to her. 'She's a one,' she would say admiringly to Hector. 'She can put anything over on everybody!' Hector would nod his head, half with pride, half with awful misgiving. At mealtimes, though, he would look a little wistful when sounds of hilarity came from below the dining-room floor; sometimes he could make out Auntie Robbo's deep bay of laughter, Mary's shrieks, and the giggles of the cook and housemaid. And when Mrs. Burston looked up fretfully to say: 'What a dreadful noise!' and Brinsley, passing his hand across his brow, took another aspirin, Hector would have given anything to be able to leave their dismal table and run down to be with Auntie Robbo. It didn't bother Pete and Sando; they liked the silent mealtimes; it gave them more time to eat. And eat they did, stolidly and seriously, from the time they sat down till it was time to get up again; they both felt that every good meal might be the last of its kind. It quite worried old Mrs. Burston. 'Don't you think they might hurt themselves?' she asked Auntie Robbo.

'Growing boys,' said Auntie Robbo airily, 'will be growing boys, you know.'

Certainly they grew; you could see a difference almost every day; already the hollows in Pete's cheeks were beginning to fill out and Sando's stomach was taking on a new rotundity.

Except for making the cook laugh too much, Auntie Robbo kept well within the bounds of her new character as the governess Miss Comrie. She 'yes, sir-ed,' and 'yes, madam-ed' the Burstons, she moved about quiet and stately as a ghost, she kept the boys loudly to order when anyone was there to see, and she performed such duties as she conceived might be Miss Comrie's with great diligence. The funny thing was that the more conscientious she was, the more it annoyed Brinsley Burston. He was always getting nasty turns, the quiet way she slipped into a room or floated round the turn of a passage. Once he nearly died: he opened the linen-cupboard door and there was Auntie Robbo, still and musing among the clean sheets. Then he thought there was always something mocking in her servility. He hated to meet her eye when he had to talk to her; he was afraid she might wink. As the days wore on he found the situation becoming not more but less bearable. Not only Auntie Robbo; not only the rough nasty children; there was his mother. You would almost have thought she was conspiring against him too, she behaved so unreasonably. She had taken a great fancy to her grandsons. She always had them with her when she felt well enough, and she was never tired of talking about them to Brinsley. She had all their careers mapped out - Hector was destined for the ministry, Alexander was to be a soldier, of course, and Peter - dear Peter - he was so clever, she thought he would be a great success at the bar. Every day she wrote a long letter of appreciation and advice to her daughter-in-law - which letters Brinsley had to extract from the post-box in the hall and destroy. He did not dare to look ahead to the frightful future consequences of his deception; the present was full of terrors enough.

And then when he had endured torment for a week, suddenly the whole thing didn't matter to him any more. He woke up with frightful pains in his stomach and a splitting headache: violent indigestion. He'd had indigestion ever since they came; nothing mattered any more except that the thing must stop and the house be rid of the whole gang of them. His health had got to be considered. He must have been mad that night on the train to have fallen in with such a plan. He had been mad for a whole week, but he would not be mad any more. He would be strong. He didn't even care what his mother might say to him when she found out.

He beckoned Auntie Robbo into his sitting-room during the morning.

'Yes, sir, coming, sir,' said Auntie Robbo, dropping a pile of children's clothes in the passage and stepping over them.

Brinsley grimaced and grew red. When he had shut the door behind her he said carefully: 'Miss Comrie - I mean

Madam whoever-you-are - this has got to stop.'

'Don't we give satisfaction, sir?' twinkled Auntie Robbo.

'That's just it,' said Brinsley indignantly. 'Surely you can see how attached my mother is becoming to these boys, these street urchins...'

'She could adopt them,' began Auntie Robbo reflectively. 'Wouldn't that be nice...?'

'No,' shouted Brinsley Burston. 'No, no. I hate the sight of them. They're awful. They make a noise. They torture me.'

Auntie Robbo felt sorry for him suddenly, and sick of the whole situation too. She dropped her governessy tones, and said in her natural voice: 'I think you're quite right, of course. This couldn't go on forever. I ought to have seen that. It's time I took this pack of children off your hands. To tell you the truth this business hasn't turned out quite as I hoped it would. The children don't seem to be enjoying it as one would have wished - at least not Hector. Still, I think it has done the other three good, don't you? The food and so on.'

Brinsley mopped his brow, relieved that she was going to go.

'But how is it to be done?' asked Auntie Robbo. 'I mean, we can't just go.'

Brinsley looked distraught.

'Give me a day or two,' said Auntie Robbo briskly. 'We're sure to think of something - or something will turn up.'

'All right,' said Brinsley sullenly. 'Only I'm sure there's *no* way out of this mess.'

Auntie Robbo shrugged her shoulders and left him.

As she closed the door, her brow knit in a frown, her eyes abstracted, she was bitterly rueing a lifetime of getting into scrapes and the impossibility of getting out of them easily. This one seemed quite as provokingly impossible as any she could remember. Stupid, too. She concluded that she must be getting old. She did not blame Brinsley, for she had known all along what kind of person he was.

'Oh, Miss Comrie!' It was old Mrs. Burston's plaintive voice. She came out of the drawing-room.

'Yes,' said Auntie Robbo, absorbed in her own thoughts.

'I am expecting a visitor tomorrow for lunch. An old friend of mine from Egypt. You know my husband and I were in Egypt before the war?'

'No,' said Auntie Robbo. She looked so deeply disinterested that Mrs. Burston went on talking from sheer nervousness.

'Yes, it was very nice, but very hot. We saw the Pyramids - and the Sphinx. Very pretty...' Mrs. Burston's voice trailed away uneasily. Auntie Robbo's expression had put her in mind of the Sphinx, that horrid great lump of stone that she and her husband had ridden such a long way into the desert to see.

'Well?' said Auntie Robbo.

'Oh, yes. It was about Mrs. Bishop. She is coming to lunch tomorrow. I want you to see that the children wash their hands and brush their hair properly. Ask them not to eat so much. I'm sure it can't be good for them. And don't you think it would be nice if they wore those pretty little suits they had on the day you came? The velvet ones with the pearl buttons.'

'No,' said Auntie Robbo, 'to be quite frank, I don't,' and she walked off down the passage, pausing to tap the barometer and rattle the sticks in the umbrella stand.

Mrs. Burston watched her in amazement, her mouth hanging open. It was only when she got back to the drawing-room that she realized how upset she was; she collapsed into her armchair moaning for Brinsley.

The truth was that, of a sudden, at the moment of shutting Brinsley Burston's sitting-room door, Auntie Robbo had sloughed off the character of Miss Comrie and become herself again. That was why she was so unmindful of old Mrs. Burston; that was why she left the pile of children's clothes in the hall where she had dropped them; and that was why, too, in the evening she put on her purple gown with the diamond tassels as a matter of course, her rings and her brooches, and sailed down to her kitchen supper.

'Lord love you,' cried the cook, considerably startled.

'And you,' replied Auntie Robbo with a bland smile. 'Ah! Kidneys sautés. How delicious!'

The kitchen was too flabbergasted to offer further comment. And even Mary, though she was 'in the know' about Auntie Robbo and longed to run her fingers over the shining taffeta and ask if the tassels were real diamonds, was too much surprised to say anything.

Afterwards Auntie Robbo wandered upstairs to the drawing-room, and sitting down opposite old Mrs. Burston began a conversation about Egypt, which she explained she had passed six times on her way to and from New Zealand.

Whether it was Auntie Robbo's witch-like eye that mesmerized them, or the effect of her gown, Brinsley Burston and his mother found themselves replying as if she had been an honoured guest. Brinsley hastened to fetch another cup and pour out coffee for her.

But after Auntie Robbo had ambled away to bed, they both succumbed to crises of the nerves; they discussed the governess far into the night. Brinsley explained that he thought Miss Comrie had gone mad, but his mother was inclined to think that she was a successful jewel thief who could no longer resist showing off her spoils. That gave Brinsley a horrible shock, for he saw that it might well be the real truth about Auntie Robbo. Why else should she have attached herself to him in the train in such a peculiar way? To gain entry into the house? And hadn't he seen her pick the lock of a trunk with a hairpin? He was so agitated that he suggested ringing up the police at once.

'No,' said his mother, 'think of the children. I think it will be best to wait till Mrs. Bishop comes. She will tell us what to do. She has seen a great deal of the world, you know. Oh, dear, oh, dear! We mustn't provoke her, Brinsley. Promise to do nothing to provoke her. She may have a pistol.'

Brinsley paled.

Before they retired, he was sent to collect all the valuables and every piece of plate in the house, in order that his mother could have them safely under lock and key in her own room.

Meanwhile Auntie Robbo was sitting in the boys' bedroom,

eating liquorice drops and discussing the situation.

'You do see, don't you?' she said for about the twentieth time. 'I mean we really can't stay here any longer.'

'That's right,' agreed Sando benignly.

'It's getting awfully dull,' Hector said. 'We can't do anything without that Brinsley telling us not to do it. And if he doesn't want us, I'm sure we don't want him.'

Then Sando thought of something else.

'I don't mind staying,' he said. 'It's better than your aunt's.'

'Yes, it is,' Pete agreed, 'but we've got to be sensible, Sando. What Auntie Robbo says is right. They might put us in clink if we stayed on here.'

'Would they now?' asked Auntie Robbo with interest. 'I never thought of that.'

Hector saw that she was almost attracted by the idea of prison, never having been there, so he cried quickly: 'Then it's all settled; we're going.'

'I know, dear Hector.' Auntie Robbo helped herself plaintively to the last liquorice drop. 'But it's not as simple as that. We can't just walk away. Think of poor Brinsley left in the soup; and old Mrs. Burston has taken such a fancy to us all. I feel quite worn out with worrying about it all.'

'Never mind now, Auntie Robbo,' said Hector. 'Something will turn up. It always does.'

'That's right,' agreed Sando.

'You're dear boys; so helpful,' murmured Auntie Robbo, and considerably cheered she went off to her own room and her usual peaceful night's rest.

CHAPTER ELEVEN

The next morning something did turn up: Mrs. Bishop in her car. Not that this was an unexpected event, but Auntie Robbo at any rate had forgotten all about it until, coming in from the garden with the children, she saw a green car parked outside the stables.

'Somebody to lunch. I forgot to tell you. A Mrs. Bishop.'

She stopped, frowning. 'Hector, you know this car gives me a funny feeling. Haven't we seen it somewhere before?'

Hector looked puzzled. Auntie Robbo knew nothing about cars and ordinarily never gave one a second glance because she wasn't interested in them.

'It's only a Morris,' said Sando. 'There's hundreds like that on the road.'

'Is there?' said Auntie Robbo, disappointed. 'But not

exactly the same, surely.'

She went up to the car, looking closely at it, and suddenly gave a cry of triumph. 'There you are! I knew it! Look, I did that myself, I did that with my hammer.' She pointed to various marks on the bonnet, where it had evidently been dented and bashed.

Hector was beside her in a moment, peering about the car. It couldn't be, it was impossible - and yet it really did seem to be Merlissa Benck's car! The car they had left, damaged and out of action, in the harness room at Nethermuir.

'She's had it mended,' said Auntie Robbo gloomily.

'And painted. Remember, it used to be blue.' Hector danced with excitement. He saw a suitcase on the back seat. It was covered with labels; the latest one bore the name of an hotel in Edinburgh and underneath was written 'Mrs. Bishop.' Others were more flamboyant, with coloured pictures of palms and deserts, Egyptian labels, French labels, London labels. And on the corner of one of these, the first part of the name plastered over, appeared what Hector had been looking for - the one word BENCK!

'It is!' he whispered to Auntie Robbo. 'It's her.'

They looked at each other in bewilderment.

'She's found us out!'

'She's followed us!'

'Under a different name!'

'Disguised, perhaps!'

They were awestruck by the cleverness of their enemy. 'What are we going to do?'

Sando and Pete and Mary fidgeted with curiosity; they peered at the car but could make nothing out of it. They strained their ears to catch the whispering of Auntie Robbo and Hector.

'What's up?' cried Sando at last, unable to contain himself. 'Is it stolen?'

'S-s-sh!' hissed Auntie Robbo. 'Listen. We must get away from here. Right away. As far as possible. At once. Now I'll go and get our things from the house. You stay here. Keep out of sight - especially Hector.'

The children retreated into the stable where, crouched in the darkness of a stall, Hector told them a little about Merlissa Benck. They were thrilled and indignant. Sando was quite willing to go and tackle her at once. The idea of wanting to put anybody like Auntie Robbo in a mad-house. Why, she was a public benefactor.

'All the same,' said Pete shrewdly, 'I bet Brinsley Burston would like to see her in a mad-house.'

Hector hadn't thought of that; it set him shivering in the gloom of the stable.

However, at that moment the sunlit door was darkened and there was Auntie Robbo back safe. Her little green shooting cap sat askew on top of her untidy hair, and she held her wicker case, overflowing with clothes, clasped in her arms.

'H-s-s-st. Come on.'

They tiptoed out of the stable.

'I say,' said Sando, grinning hopefully up at her. 'I could

drive that car. The baker used to let me have a shot at his, and it was a Morris.'

'How clever of you, Sando. I expect we had better borrow it then. We really must hurry.'

Hector was about to protest, but already Auntie Robbo had hoisted Merlissa Benck's suitcase out into the yard, and substituted her own. Sando scrambled in at the wheel and switched on the engine. Auntie Robbo leaped in and they all bundled after, even as the car began to move forwards.

'The back drive!' cried Auntie Robbo. 'Don't go in front of the house.'

Sando jerked the wheel round towards the tradesmen's entrance. They bumped over a flower bed, swung round a mass of rhododendrons, and were mercifully screened from the house.

At that very moment in the drawing-room, Merlissa Benck, tense with a sudden suspicion, was asking the Burstons to describe their queer governess to her. It couldn't be, and yet... Had her prey been snatched ruthlessly from beneath her nose, only to be placed beneath it again, cooked and dished?

The back drive was narrow and tortuous, giving onto an equally narrow though not quite so tortuous lane. When Sando had navigated these, he felt himself a much better driver and he opened out a bit on the broad main road. They fairly sped along, and Stirling was soon left far behind in a cloud of stour. Pete, sitting in front beside Sando, smiled grimly. Auntie Robbo leaned forward to cheer, though she and Hector and Mary were still shaken and breathless and

rather mixed up in the back seat. Pete told her to sit back and
not disturb the driver. As a matter of fact, Sando was not in
the least disturbed; he saw nothing but the leaping road and
heard nothing but the purr of his engine. A bland smile was
fixed on his face, and his eyes stared serenely ahead.

'I tell you,' said Hector feebly from under the wicker case.
'It *is* different from horse-stealing. Auntie Robbo, you've got
to listen to reason.'

Sando blew the horn vigorously on a corner and Auntie
Robbo leaned forward to help him.

'Anyway, they hang you for horse-stealing,' shouted
Hector.

'Poof, not in my day,' she replied.

'Well, a horse is different,' he persisted. 'It can find its way
home again. Borrowing a car is a very serious crime.'

Auntie Robbo gave an airy wave of her hand, and Hector
sat back in despair; he had been carrying on the one-sided
argument ever since they got into the car. But at this point
Mary unexpectedly perked up and came to his support.

'The poliss'll have something to say,' she announced,
'when they catch Sando driving. He hasn't got a licence.'

'Licence or no licence,' remarked Auntie Robbo blandly,
'he seems to be doing very nicely.'

The words 'poliss' and 'licence' had somehow penetrated
to Sando, above the noise of the engine, and they must
have meant something to him, in the midst of his glorious
indifference, for at that moment he chose to swing the car off
the busy main road at about forty miles an hour. Fortunately

there *was* a side road there, but they turned the corner so abruptly that a mudguard was left behind. Pete's nose bled from hitting it against the windscreen. Auntie Robbo pitched on top of Mary, almost squashing the life out of her, and Hector and the contents of the wicker case mixed themselves up on the floor.

When everybody had recovered from this mishap, they found they were bumping along a narrow country road, pitted with holes and tussocked with grass; on either side, so close that they could almost have fallen out into them, were deep lush ditches filled with rose bushes and topped with hawthorn.

'Gee, that was a near thing,' Sando kept saying gleefully. 'A close shave.'

'There'll be a closer one if we meet anything on this road.' Pete leaned over to sound the horn as they came to a corner, and in doing so dripped blood on the steering wheel. Sando was furious. 'Get off, I'm doing this. Stop your dripping. Put a key down your neck.'

'Look out.' There was a yell from the back seat, and they were all flung on their noses as Sando applied the brakes hard.

'I *was* looking,' he said with dignity.

Ahead, completely blocking the narrow road, was a pony and cart. An outstrapulous equipage. The pony was a moth-eaten piebald, but pleasant-looking; the cart was covered over with worn canvas stretched on hoops, and hung about with bunches of glinting, brand-new tin pails. Sitting up on front with his feet on the shafts was a little thin man, yellow as a smoked haddock, with beery yellow moustaches and jaundiced eyes. He did not seem in the least surprised or put out by the situation. He just sat there, cocking his head a little, as if he heard distant music, until Pete stopped blowing the horn.

'Ye'll hae tae back,' he said then. 'Ye can dae it easier nor me in your lordly carriage.' Sando looked embarrassed and fiddled with the gears.

'Go on, then,' whispered Pete. 'Hae a shot at it.'

'It's a terrible long way,' he whispered back.

'What's the matter?' asked Auntie Robbo.

Sando blurted out in dismay: 'I never learned to go

backleens. I don't like to try it just here.'

Auntie Robbo poked her head out of the window. 'Wait a minute, will you? We aren't quite ready yet. We've got something to discuss.'

'Och, I'm in no hurry, your ladyship. But wan thing, *I'm* no going to back whatever the ootcome o' your discussions. The law's the law. And it says motor vehicles must aye give way to horses and cairts.'

'Does it really?'

'Aye, it does so. And if it doesna, it ought to -'

'Oh, I quite agree,' said Auntie Robbo warmly. 'Very sensible. Well, we'll see what can be done.'

She retired into the car. 'Now, Sando, what's this I hear about your not having a driving licence?'

'Didn't ye ken?' said Sando in real horror: 'I would never have done it if I'd thought that.'

'What difference does it make?'

'Well, you could clear us with the cops.'

'Oh?' said Auntie Robbo. 'Oh. Well, I don't know about that. There seems to be a good many laws about cars, far more than I imagined. Besides it *is* a disadvantage, your not knowing how to make the thing go backwards. I always said there was nothing to beat a horse and trap; anyone can make that go anywhere - back or forwards or sideways - *and* you don't need a licence or any nonsense like that.' She looked wistfully at the equipage blocking their road.

'Well, he's not making his go backwards, anyway,' Pete pointed out. He tooted the horn derisively.

'That's just duggedness,' said Mary. 'He looks an awful dugged man. So does his horse.'

'It's not a bad-like beast,' said Auntie Robbo thoughtfully. 'I'm sure that I could make it go backwards.' She got out of the car and went up to the tinker and his cart.

'I'm sorry to say we find we can't go backwards,' she announced.

'You ca-a-an't?'

'No, quite impossible. Out of the question. But I'll tell you what. If you can drive a car, you could have ours, and make it go backwards. We'd take the horse and cart in exchange.'

The tinker leaned back in astonishment. 'Oh, ye wad, wad ye?'

'You see, it's a stolen car.'

'Ho-oo-oo,' cried the tinker, leaning further back.

'And we haven't got a licence.'

The tinker just managed to save himself from toppling into his cart. He drew a deep breath, and then, waggling a dirty forefinger at Auntie Robbo, said severely: 'Ye ought tae be ashamed o' yourself, auld wife, downright ashamed, pitting temptation in the way of an honest man.'

Auntie Robbo was a little nonplussed. She beckoned to the children.

'It's a fine turn-out, isn't it? I like it much better than Merlissa Benck's. But he doesn't want to exchange.'

Sando said with some disgust: 'Why, that car's worth ten times as much as his old horse.'

'Perhaps he can't drive,' Pete suggested.

'I can so then,' flashed the tinker. 'I used to hae a motor-bike.'

'No, it's because it's stolen,' said Auntie Robbo. 'He says he's an honest man.'

They all stared up at the tinker. He plucked the ends of his moustache primly.

Hector burst out excitedly. 'I know. He could change the number plate. I've read about it. It's quite easy. Then the police don't know it's a stolen car.'

'Of course,' cried Auntie Robbo. 'Why didn't we think of that before?' Her eye lighted on a little pot of tar hanging from the tail of the cart. She unhooked it, and went up to Merlissa Benck's car. 'Quite simple,' she said, blotting out the numbers with a single sweep of the brush.

She stepped back, and they all looked up at the tinker again - this time hopefully.

He just shook his head: 'It isna simple at all. I've hid some experience wi' ma motor-bike.'

A few minutes before they had not even set eyes on the pony and cart; now it seemed the most desirable object on earth. Especially Hector wanted it; he would have done anything to be quit of Merlissa Benck's car.

'It *is* a nice little cart,' said Mary. 'And the horse wouldn't bite. He's got no teeth.'

'He's been a good horse in his day,' sighed Auntie Robbo.

The tinker coughed rheumily and stared into space.

'I'll tell ye what,' he said at last. 'I can see there's more in this than meets the eye. Ye're in a fix, that's what it is, a bit of a jam. I've aye been willing to help a body in a jam, never knowing when I might be in wan meself. Well, what d'you say to making me an offer for my powny and cairt? The car can just bide whaur it is. Least said, soonest mended.'

Everybody was very pleased.

Now it had to be decided just how much the pony was worth. The tinker swore he had paid twenty pounds for it, but Auntie Robbo argued that that must have been at least twenty years ago. However, she agreed that she might give that much if the cart was thrown in as well, with all its contents and fittings. Not that Auntie Robbo wanted the 'contents and fittings' - or even thought what they might be - but, rash and reckless as a rule when spending money, in horse-dealings she liked to think she was as sharp as a knife. It was one of her traditions. She and the tinker bargained fiercely while Hector looked anxiously down the lane for signs of policemen and Merlissa Benck on their track, and Sando kicked his heels angrily and looked longingly at the abandoned car. But at last agreement was reached - fifteen pounds. Then it had to be decided how the money was to be paid. Auntie Robbo had not fifteen pounds in cash on her, and the tinker said naturally that he couldn't take a cheque.

'I like the look of ye, lady,' he said. 'It isn't that I don't trust ye. But I can't be doing with banks, I can't, and that's the truth. I never give them trade if I can help it.'

Eventually he suggested that he should go along with them until Auntie Robbo could get the money from a bank herself; and with that they had to be content.

CHAPTER TWELVE

There was a deal of trouble in getting the pony and cart turned in the narrow lane. One wheel went into the ditch. A bunch of pails, slipping their moorings, fell clattering in all directions. The pony bucked and stamped, showing there was life in his old bones yet. And the tinker swore bitterly. Hector shut his ears against the swearing; Auntie Robbo listened politely, trying to make out what it meant; nobody else seemed to notice.

At last they were set four-square on the road with the horse's nose pointing in the right direction. Auntie Robbo led the way, with the tinker striding along so that he breathed hard to keep up with her. She discovered that he had been in New Zealand in his youth, and this provided her with one of her favourite topics of conversation. The tinker hardly got a word in edgeways.

Behind them the pony came ambling, stopping to chew at the ditches sometimes. Hector and Pete sat up in front of the cart, handling the whip and reins between them.

Hector was so happy that he made up a little song.

'Giddy-up, giddy-up, my bonny black mare. Lift up your legs - the other rein, Pete, you sap - or we'll never get there! No, we'll never get there!'

He flourished the whip over the pony's ears, or flicked it among the overhanging beech leaves. Once he cracked it by mistake and the pony looked round at him cannily. The tinker jumped and grew quite pale under his dirt. He seemed to be a nervous little man.

Inside the cart Mary was crawling about making the most astonishing discoveries among their new possessions. She held them up for Hector and Pete to see - a tartan tea-caddy, a bag of rags, a broken soup-plate, a girdle encrusted with grease and dust, 'but quite good still,' she pointed out.

'Phew,' sniffed Pete, who had incautiously stuck his head near to look at the girdle. 'It smells.'

'Yes, everything does,' said Mary. 'It needs a good clean.'

'It's a very queer smell,' said Hector. 'Not an ordinary smell.'

He was right. A few minutes later Mary pounced with a scream on a bunch of half-cured rabbitskins that had been lying hid in a corner. She flung them out of the back of the cart.

'Hi?' came Sando's protesting voice. He had been

slouching along behind, kicking tussocks of grass and spitting forcefully, and generally showing nobody in particular how disgusted he was by the pony and cart transaction. Imagine anyone preferring to ride along the back lanes in a smelly cart pulled by a broken-down horse when they could be motoring along the broad main road in comfort and style? But it was not in Sando to sulk for long. His slouch became less pronounced and his spit more infrequent. He caught up with the cart and began hanging onto its tail. When the rabbit-skins came flying over his head, he hoisted himself up and joined his sister under the canvas hood. He didn't stay there long - though he sympathized with Mary's enthusiasm for digging among the rubbish - but came out to the fresh air in front. And before he knew it he was holding the reins, and Pete and Hector were showing him how to drive a horse. He began to like it.

They were on the old main road to the Highlands, the tinker told them. Sometimes it was narrow and overgrown, little more than a tunnel between dense hedges and overhanging trees; sometimes it ran stonily over a bit of moor; sometimes it became quite respectable, passing through a farmsteading or a village; and then for a mile or two it would turn into the real main road again, tar-macadamed and telegraph-wired, bristling with signposts and traffic signals. But always it became as they had first found it, splitting away from the main road to seclusion and neglect. It disappeared at last into a cornfield, but the tinker said they would find it again on the other side. Meanwhile they camped on the last traces of

it - to eat and to sleep.

They hadn't eaten since the morning, but they had been too excited in what had been happening to them to notice it much. The tinker fished out of the debris in his cart a frying pan, a string of onions, and various paper and newspaper packages. Under his direction wood was gathered and a fire lit, and when it was going bravely he set about making the supper. The rest sat round in a tired circle watching him. He put lumps of lard into the frying pan, and then lumps of onion sawed up by his jack-knife, and then he kept sprinkling oatmeal on top, stirring vigorously with a bit of stick until all was a sort of lumpy burnt fried porridge.

'It's ready,' cried the tinker triumphantly.

The children ate with relish, for they were very hungry indeed, and washed down the mess with mugs of strong tarry tea - also the tinker's brew. But Auntie Robbo had more respect for her stomach.

The tinker saw her toying uneasily with her plateful.

'Good, isna it?' he said, fixing her with his jaundiced eye.

Auntie Robbo said nothing.

'They ca' it skirl-i'-the-pan, and a man micht march a day and a night on a stomach-load o' this, and never feel a want.'

'Oh,' said Auntie Robbo.

The tinker began to cut bread with a flat dirty thumb pressed into the loaf and an onion-stained knife. Auntie Robbo got up quietly and shimmered off into the dusk, carrying her plate. When she was out of sight she found a big rabbit hole and buried her skirl-i'-the-pan, plate and all.

Then she hurried back up the road until she came to a farm, where, without much difficulty, she got a nice satisfying meal of ham and eggs and milk and gingerbread. She felt a little mean about this, but took back to the children a basket of eggs and some new-baked scones.

'Eggs!' exclaimed the tinker when she came up. 'Ye havena been buying eggs?'

'Oh, yes,' said Auntie Robbo. 'For the breakfast. I got them at that farm we passed.'

'*Buying* eggs?' exclaimed the tinker. 'I never heard the like. And a hen-hoose right forrent your nose, wumman!' He pointed to the black-tarred roof that topped the dyke of the next field, and spat expressively.

Auntie Robbo looked shocked. 'You're not suggesting I should steal?'

The tinker cackled. 'I thocht it was a habit, your ladyship. Beg your pardon. Ganging off wi' a car is jest in the day's wark, but it seems a bit hen's egg sticks in yer ladylike gullet.'

'That's exactly it,' replied Auntie Robbo. 'I'm so glad you see. It means that you aren't quite devoid of a moral sense. Good-night all.'

Auntie Robbo stalked off to the cart, and disappeared head first through the canvas flaps. Shortly tins and pots, insulting remarks, bits of food and rags came flying out as she prepared her bed. The tinker muttered angrily but did not protest. And in a little while there was no sound from the cart but a light placid snore. The clouds of midges danced in the evening air, now high, now low, to the rhythm of it.

For a while the children and the tinker sat on round the fire. With Auntie Robbo gone, he became garrulous and expansive - spinning many a wild tale about his adventures and progress. Sometimes Hector and Pete caught each other's eye, or stirred uneasily at some particularly outrageous lie. But not Sando, simple soul; he listened raptly, and came pat with applause or enthusiasm or amazement just when the tinker needed them.

But his talk wasn't altogether unprofitable, for he passed on a lot of hints about camping grounds and poaching and lighting fires and selling tin pails. He and Sando were still discussing pails when Mary crept away to lie beside Auntie Robbo, and Hector and Pete fell asleep where they sat.

CHAPTER THIRTEEN

Hector woke with the sun in his eyes - an early sun, all brightness and no warmth. A dirty quilt had been thrown over Pete and himself as they lay beside the ashes of the fire. The ashes were cold now, and the quilt had a thick beard of dew. Hector was stiff and chilled. He stretched his legs, which he had been hugging all night for warmth, and lifted his head. There was no sign of the tinker and Sando. Actually they had slept under the cart, where the tinker's snoring had had no effect on the calm slumbers of Auntie Robbo above, but had wakened Mary in a sweat of fear. She had listened and quaked and prickled with horror, imagining it was some wild country beast come to get them, a bull or a stag or a bogle.

The tinker had roused Sando an hour before Hector woke,

and had taken him off to collect wood and have a lesson in setting snares.

Hector had a look at Pete, lying curled up beside him, dead asleep; then another look around him. The world was marvellously fresh and brilliant. The grass smelled as he had never known grass could smell; he could see a little birch tree with gleaming white stalk in the sunlight and a shower of minute gleaming leaves; and the birds sang their loudest and longest as if they believed nobody was there to hear them. And besides the bird's singing, there was a modest gobbling, tinkling song from the little burn where they had got water the night before.

That was enough for Hector. He leaped up with a whoop, dragging the coverlet with him. Pete clutched vaguely and grumpily at the empty air, then jumped up too. As he ran after Hector, there was the sound of rending canvas and Auntie Robbo popped out of the top of the cart like a jack-in-the-box. She still wore her little green cap, and her hair rose wild and woolly around it.

'A beautiful morning?' She yawned and stretched - more rending of canvas. 'Dear me, supposing it rained? Mary, remind me to get a new roof.'

Down by the burn, Hector and Pete had stripped off their clothes, shivering. But soon they were thrashing about and ducking each other in the stinging clear water so that they forgot to be cold. Then they raced round in circles to dry.

Auntie Robbo came down to make her toilet. She washed very heartily, dipping her face, blowing like a grampus. Then she did her hair and retired behind some gorse bushes to change her dress and little green hat for her yachting outfit. It gave her a pang to have to wear the wrong clothes; she wished she had brought her riding habit, but it could not be helped. When she emerged at last, spruce and clean, it was to find the tinker lecturing Hector and Pete for bathing without anything on.

At the sight of Auntie Robbo he stopped short. He gaped at her change of clothes, then recovered himself. 'It's scandalous. It's no dacent. The law's the law, and the law says...'

'Oh, nonsense,' said Auntie Robbo airily. 'There's no law against taking a bath in the morning. Didn't you know? Perhaps not, perhaps not.'

The tinker gulped indignantly. He picked up his bundle of sticks and went off to the camp. 'And weemen wearing men's caps!' he muttered as he began to start the fire. That really offended him as much as anything. The glassy peak and gold braid of Auntie Robbo's yachting cap had such an air of authority about it.

Breakfast passed off peacefully enough. The tinker made porridge, which the children ate. And then there were the eggs, lightly done by Auntie Robbo, in the teeth of the tinker's opposition. Everybody had two except the tinker, who only got one. Auntie Robbo had three.

'Weemen!' said the tinker bitterly.

By nine o'clock the pony was harnessed to the cart and, after making a difficult detour through fields and round a wood, they found the old road again and marched along it as quickly as they could, for they wanted to reach Perth that day.

Auntie Robbo and the tinker no longer walked ahead together. They were hardly on speaking terms. The final rupture had come when Auntie Robbo had insisted on abandoning all the lumber which she had thrown out of the cart the night before. She said she had bought it and if she chose to leave it in a field that was her business. The tinker said she hadn't paid for it yet and there were a lot of valuables among it and, supposing he didn't get his money, it would be a dead loss. In the end Mary settled the business by picking out one or two things which she thought would be useful to them - such as the tartan tea-caddy, some china, a paraffin can, and allowing the tinker to pack up what he wanted in an old quilt to be taken away with him when he left. Everybody thought this a good idea except the tinker, who mainly wanted something to be aggrieved about.

It was afternoon before they reached Perth, hungry and rather footsore. But Auntie Robbo said they must go and do their shopping at once because there was such a lot to buy. She had made a list, as they walked along, in consultation with the children. Besides, they would have to hurry to catch the bank. They had halted in a field just on the outskirts. So the tinker was left in charge with instructions to water the horse and make a fire and he would get his money when they came back.

Shopping with Auntie Robbo was neither tiresome nor

dull. She always knew exactly what she wanted, and she never asked the price of anything. And the children had only to decide the most delightful questions - like what colour of paint for the cart, or whether they wanted their blankets plain or striped. Striped it was. They rushed from shop to shop: bedding, a Primus stove, pots and pans, provisions, new canvas for the cart, a cookery book for Mary, oats for the horse, and an Inverness cape to save Auntie Robbo's yachting suit.

Half-way through they fortified themselves with a large high tea; Auntie Robbo had no intention of returning to the tinker's cooking. Then they hired a van to take them and their purchases back to the camp.

Darkness was falling when they reached the field. Near the cart the horse was cropping peacefully and there was a heartening glow from a little fire, carefully stoked down with sods of turf. But there was no sign of the tinker. At first they didn't miss him in the bustle of unloading the stuff and paying off the van-man. But then they began to look around for him. They called, they whistled, they walked along the dykes. No tinker. Auntie Robbo was worried in case he had had an accident; and Hector almost wept because he felt they had not treated him very kindly.

'He's maybe off poaching,' suggested Sando.

'Very likely,' agreed Auntie Robbo. 'Anyway, we can't do anything more tonight.'

She went into the cart, hauling some of the new bedding after her; and there on a nail where she had hung her gold watch that morning was a grubby note.

'The poliss was here. Look out. I'm off.'

The gold watch was off too. And so - when Auntie Robbo looked into her wicker case - were her binoculars. 'Was it worth much?' asked Sando anxiously.

'No - no more than was his due. At least I hope not.' She reached over quickly and picked up Mary's tartan tea-caddy. It rattled heartily like a well-filled money-box. Auntie Robbo smiled. 'Isn't it lucky he didn't find this?' She opened the box and showed a tangle of brooches and rings and bangles and pendants, flashing and rich in the rusted old tin. 'I'm so fond of them.' She sighed happily, fishing out a ring or two and

slipping them on her finger. 'You said this tea-caddy would be useful, Mary. How clever of you!'

'But why didn't the tinker wait for his money?' asked Pete. 'It was daft, going off like that. It'll be a job selling the things he took.'

'Oh, I expect he thought a bird in the hand was worth two in the bush,' said Auntie Robbo. 'He was a most impulsive, thoughtless critter.'

'I don't think it was that at all,' said Hector sombrely. 'I think it was the police. He thought we'd be arrested for stealing Merlissa Benck's car, and I think he's right.'

There was a stunned silence.

'The poliss were here,' breathed Pete, as if he had just realized it.

'Yes, the note does say that,' agreed Auntie Robbo. 'But it mayn't be true. Anyhow, does it matter?'

The children assured her fervently that it did. Sando related one or two lurid stories about his stepfather and the 'ways of the poliss'.

'They don't know we're here, that's one thing,' Mary pointed out.

'Not yet,' said Sando. 'But give them time. They'll be out with their bloodhounds and their plainclothes men the morn. The poliss get to know everything.'

Auntie Robbo looked amazed. 'Surely not,' she said. 'Don't you think Sando's a little superstitious?' she appealed to Hector.

'No,' he replied downrightly.

It wasn't the police that worried him so much; but behind the police he saw looming the awful figure of Merlissa Benck, relentless and stupid, bent on clapping Auntie Robbo into an asylum and himself into a public school.

'No,' he repeated, 'the best thing we can do is to get away from here at once.'

'Now?' protested Auntie Robbo. 'But it's time to go to bed.'

They assured her that she could sleep in the cart, and they would do all the work.

'That will be delightful,' Auntie Robbo agreed. 'It will be such a surprise waking up in the morning. And I shan't mind the bumps at all. I'm a very good traveller. I can sleep through anything.'

So she lay down and the children packed all the stuff they had bought round about her. The horse was harnessed and they got onto the road again. They set off at a snail's pace, for they were all weary, the horse as much as anybody. At last they got round about the town. Slowly the bright lights receded until they were a haze on the southern horizon. The moon came up showing they were on a moor. And when at last they had crossed it, gaining the friendly shadows and darkness of hills on the other side, they drew up the cart, fished out blankets from around the snoring Auntie Robbo, and dropped to sleep among the heather.

CHAPTER FOURTEEN

'I can't get it *quite* right,' mumbled Auntie Robbo. She was perched on her shooting-stick by the side of a burn with a sketching block on her knee. A paint-brush was clenched in her teeth like the knife of an ancient warrior; there was a green gash on her cheek and her hands were dabbled with crimson.

'I ought to have an easel,' she said plaintively, and fixed her attention again on the old mossy bridge that spanned the burn a hundred yards farther up. It leaned drunkenly on its twin chunky arches; ferns and briars protruded from it in bewildering profusion; a waterfall splashed behind it. It was a difficult subject to paint, and Auntie Robbo had made it more difficult by putting in an imaginary cow paddling in the burn. There was something wrong with the cow; Auntie

Robbo admitted that to herself. But still she would not forgo it because all the pictures she had ever seen of Highland scenery had had a cow in the foreground - or a stag; but a stag was even worse.

In her despair, she called up Pete and Hector from the burnside where they had been trying to catch a trout.

'It's the water,' sighed Auntie Robbo. 'It splashes such a lot. How can one paint splashes?'

Pete and Hector gazed critically at the picture.

'There's something wrong with the cow,' said Hector.

'Oh, I know,' said Auntie Robbo touchily.

'Splashes?' said Pete, taking Auntie Robbo's brush and churning it round in blue paint. 'That's easy. You just splash.' He waved the brush - and a shower of blue paint flew towards the picture. Most of it landed on Auntie Robbo.

'You've spoilt it! Oh, I was getting on so nicely - '

'Splashes!' cried Pete exultantly. 'That's the way to do splashes. But you've got to leave white bits too. Look, I could do it for you - '

Auntie Robbo hugged her paint-box to her breast. 'Have you ever painted before, Pete?'

'Not yet. They wouldn't let me at the school. They said I messed up their paint-boxes.'

'That's what paint-boxes are for,' said Hector, throwing a stone into the burn. 'Come on, Auntie Robbo, let's make a fishing rod. This burn is simply teeming with trout.'

Auntie Robbo was in truth a little bored with sketching the old bridge and the imaginary cow; but she surrendered her

paint-box reluctantly. She never got it back again, as it turned out.

Pete began to daub blissfully. Hector and Auntie Robbo moved downstream searching for a straight bit of hazel; they disappeared round the bend. Pete never noticed; he went on daubing - hills, sky, heather, bridges, cows, little men, the roof of the cart down below in the glen, birds, bogles. He almost finished the paper. Darkness was coming down. The paint-box was flooded and streaked with gorgeous colours. He cleaned it lovingly in the burn, tucked his pictures under his arm, and climbed down to the camp.

It was a very nice camp now; it was a fortnight since the evening when they had fled from the police at Perth and great changes had taken place. The piebald pony, cropping beside the cart, was shod and sleeked and fattened so that he hardly knew himself. That had been Auntie Robbo's work. New bright green canvas roofed the cart, which had been painted yellow, with red whorls over the wheels. It looked very pretty. Like a bit of a circus that had got lost among the hills. They were camped that day in a narrow green-valleyed glen. Farther down one or two crofts and a village were just beginning to show lights. Hills rose, blackening and stolid, all around.

There was no sign of Auntie Robbo and Hector when Pete came down; they must have had success with the fishing. He did not expect to see Sando and Mary, for they had gone off down the glen earlier in the day to sell pails. Sando had developed a mania for selling pails. At first they had been too busy fleeing from Perth and the police and Merlissa Benck; and then had come the cleaning up of the camp, re-arranging their life in the open air, painting the cart, and so on. But lately Auntie Robbo had complained that the stock of tin pails left by the tinker were a nuisance; they rattled so much, hung in their bunches. Besides, the hooks which they occupied outside the cart were needed for other things - onions and paraffin. She refused to sleep with onions and paraffin. So Sando had begun selling the pails. He'd had practice in his apprenticeship to the baker and he did well. He remembered all that the tinker had told him about 'the tred' and he took to it like a duck to water. Often the cart left him far behind as he bargained at some wayside farm. And when the others planned a pleasant afternoon bathing in a loch or lazing on the hillside, Sando would set off with his pails. He took his sister with him sometimes, because in some mysterious way she softened the hearts of housewives. At any rate, she was obliging enough to carry half the load of pails.

Pete went into the cart to get some bread and jam. He was very hungry after painting. The inside of the cart was as greatly changed as the outside: neat and scrubbed white, their possessions ranged in shelves, and the bedding piled to make a couch. Nobody would have recognized it as the same cart which had held the tinker's rubbish of rags and broken china. Perhaps that was as well, thought Pete, remembering the police. It seemed a long way back. They had been doing so much and having such a pleasant time since then that it seemed as if it had happened to other people. The whole tenor of their life was different. Even Hector had given up moaning 'Merlissa Benck' when he had a nightmare, and if the name of Brinsley Burston had been mentioned, it is doubtful if any of them would have recognized it.

Pete had eaten six pieces of bread and jam and had almost become tired of admiring his pictures, when he was hailed from outside. It was Hector come back. He had left Auntie Robbo still fishing. Pete was glad of that, for he wanted to show off his pictures. He brought them out to the fire which Hector had kicked into a blaze. They sat close together, their heads touching. The flames danced, making the colours shift and fade.

'You see, it's a man with a sheep on his back...'

'Why has he got a sheep on his back?'

'I don't ken,' said Pete vaguely.

'But why? You must ken. You made him.'

'Och, it's a dead sheep maybe. Look, at this now - look at the bogle.'

'The paint's run,' said Hector critically.

'It's the fire.'

'No, it's all smudged. You must ha' put it down wet.'

'It's *meant* to be like that.'

'All right. Don't prod me.'

'Do you see the face?'

'Oh, yes,' breathed Hector, 'that's a terrible-like face. What an *enormous* face!'

Pete chuckled with delight. Hector gaped at the picture for a moment or two. He took a swift look round at the darkened hills; he looked upwards at the wood smoke spiralling into the pale evening sky; he edged a little closer to the fire.

'Show me the next one,' he said.

Pete showed him the next one; it was of Auntie Robbo fishing. One booted leg elegantly poised for balance; a pipe clenched between grinning teeth; and seven fish hooked on her line.

'Look, I gave her a pipe.' Pete pointed it out. 'To match her hat.'

Hector laughed. She looked so funny - more like Sherlock Holmes than Auntie Robbo. They were still laughing over this when Auntie Robbo came up to the other side of the fire.

'Look! Look at this! Look at yourself!' cried Hector leaping up. Pete would have snatched the picture if he could have. Auntie Robbo gazed solemnly at the portrait presented to her, solemnly laid her rod on the ground, solemnly said: 'That's very remarkable.'

Pete was abashed; he was sorry he had made her such a guy. He wouldn't have, if he'd thought about it.

'You see,' said Auntie Robbo, holding out her little green cap in which reposed her catch. 'There *are* seven fish. It's the second sight, that's what it is. Had you any Highland grandmothers, Pete?'

Pete looked alarmed. He snatched the picture from Hector and looked closely at it. 'There's only six fish,' he said quickly. 'Of course there are, the other one's a smudge.'

'Well, look at this, Auntie Robbo. You see, it's a man with a sheep on his back.'

'Why has he got a sheep on his back?'

'It's dead, of course. Can't you see the way the head is hanging?'

Auntie Robbo had to sit down in the firelight with them and look at all Pete's wonderful pictures. They were wonderful, Auntie Robbo admitted that. But they weren't quite right; they weren't like the Highland scenes ladies painted when she was young. Pete said he didn't think any ladies could paint. Hector said the ladies' pictures - some decorated the bedrooms at Nethermuir - were all the same, not like Pete's. They were full of cows and mountains, the same cows and the same mountains. Auntie Robbo said some had stags, and not cows. Hector said there was no difference; for stags they drew horns that branched, for cows straight ones, that was all. They were still arguing about this, when a shout came from further down the glen. It was Sando and Mary returning. Tin rattled on tin, there was a clatter of feet on the rocky path, and Mary cried out not to be left behind in the dark.

'All but two!' shouted Sando, running up to the fire.

He tossed the pails down with a triumphant clatter.

'Seven and fourpence,' gasped Mary, dancing up with money outstretched in her fist.

When the shouting and acclamation had died down a bit, Sando said he was hungry. The three round the fire looked guilty and immediately sorry. They had forgotten all about supper.

'Sit ye down, Mary,' said Auntie Robbo. 'I'll get the things out.'

'I'll gut the fish,' cried Hector.

'And I'll fry them,' said Pete cheerfully.

And when the fresh curling trout had been eaten, with a mound of scones and butter, they lay late round the fire, swilling cocoa, arguing again about stags and cows, telling stories, and looking back on yet another well-spent perfect day.

CHAPTER FIFTEEN

It was June when they reached the Caledonian Canal. The Highland summer was at its best - long, sun-filled, wind-cooled days when the sky grew only more deeply blue as the hours passed, flaring at last into splendid sunset, dying into the pale gloom of night. They got up with the sun, they went to bed with it. All the world was newly green - as if spring was in summer there - bright grass, unfurling bracken, young heather. Wild flowers crowded the ditches and burns. Hayfields and new corn shone, their short crops combed by the summer wind. Far away hills lay like static blue clouds against the bluer sky; and near at hand, sun-striped and tawny, like great beasts lapped in sleep.

The children grew brown as nuts, and Auntie Robbo, who was tolerably weatherbeaten at any time of the year, freckled like a turkey's egg. They were all supremely happy. They sampled new bathing every day, in lochans, peat-stained on the hilltops, in grey land-lochs dotted with islets and swans, and in the sea-lochs, the great arms of the sea that came feeling into the heart of the Highlands. They learned to swim. They climbed mountains. They explored caves. Mary cooked more and more expertly; Pete painted; Sando sold pails- he had had to renew his stock twice. Auntie Robbo and Hector had no particular enthusiasm; their enjoyment was spread over everything - the scenery, the pails, the weather, the painting, the lochs, and the cooking.

But this idyll - everybody happy, everything going smoothly couldn't last forever. It lasted till the day they stepped into Ross-shire. There the weather broke. That was the beginning.

It began to rain, not just ordinary rain in showers, but a wetness that crept up from the sea, grey and woolly, permeating everything. Even when they had sat huddled in the cart with dry clothes on, still the rain seemed to have seeped under their skin, into their bones. They were always shivering. They ate wetly off rain-soaked, half-cooked food. It was impossible to light a fire outside, and the little canvas-covered cart, which was their only shelter, filled with a dense fog, composed of Primus fumes and cooking, drying clothes, and wet bodies.

After an hour in this atmosphere, Auntie Robbo would suddenly leap up, upsetting everything and everybody - because of course there was hardly room to spread a hand or scratch an ear once they were all in the cart - and rush outside into the rain. She didn't really mind the wet, finding the countryside always beautiful in bad weather as in fine - and would stride up the nearest hill or round the nearest loch to air her lungs. But when she returned it would be to even greater discomfort. It was a feat they never quite achieved - drying Auntie Robbo's voluminous skirt round the Primus, or scraping the glaur off her boots without getting *some* in the blankets or the supper.

Sando was the only one of them who remained cheerful and good-tempered under these circumstances. And even in the rain he went on selling pails. He said that his business seemed to grow better, for on a fine day the farm folk might be too busy to be bothered with him, but when it rained they welcomed him as a diversion.

It rained for eight days. On the ninth, just when they had given up all hope and Auntie Robbo was confined to her bed because she didn't have a dry rag to her back, and the horse had rheumatics, and Hector a cold, and the Primus wouldn't work because it had got water in its bowl - on the ninth day the sun began to glimmer through the still-watery sky. Immediately all was bustle and hope about the camp again.

Auntie Robbo was for pushing off eastwards at once; it would be dryer there, she said. She remembered learning it in her geography book at school: Scotland; warm and wet climate on the west coast, cold and dry on the east.

'This is *cold* and wet,' objected Hector. 'I hope we aren't going to be any colder.'

'It's the damp that makes you cold. On the east coast it will be lovely, dry as a bone, sunny - not really cold - bracing!'

So they set off about mid-day when the sky had really cleared. They hung clothes and bedding about the cart to dry as they moved. The pony stepped out more briskly than he had in a week. Their way lay through narrow glens and wild hills. It was a lovely road, sometimes they passed a shepherd with a flock of sheep, or a poor croft or two back from the road, usually deserted.

The hills in this part were ranked so closely together that they were oppressive, rising out of each other's shoulders and menacing the narrow road. However, they marched along happily enough, rejoicing in the fine weather. And all went well until late in the afternoon when they came into a glen much like a score of others they had passed through that day. But this glen was dominated by a big red sandstone house. It stood at the far end of it, well back from the road. It was a very ugly house with big blank windows and silly-looking turrets and cupola surmounted by a Union Jack. It was the sort of house that ought to have been buried behind a lot of trees, but here it stood up naked and strident among the quiet hills. Beyond it rose a single stately mountain peak; and it seemed to be pushing itself forward, sneering: 'Yah, think that's grand, don't yer? But look at me! Look how much I cost! Look how grand I am. I'm a house, I am - not a blooming mountain!' It really was a horrid house.

But to one of the party at least it was a most welcome sight. Sando hallooed with joy; he wanted to go and sell his pails to it.

'You won't do any business there,' said Auntie Robbo. 'It's a shooting lodge. Empty this time of the year.'

'The flag's flying,' Sando pointed out. He was determined to sell some pails. He said they were passing fewer and fewer houses every day and it was a shame to let a big beauty like this one go. He might be able to sell them his whole stock.

Auntie Robbo was unconvinced, but quite ready to oblige Sando and break the monotony of their journey. So when they came almost up to the house, she amiably turned the pony into the drive.

The front of the house was bold and unappetizing; the back was more human, and Auntie Robbo was surprised to see a well-kept and rather charming garden, walled and tilting up to the hill behind. The clanging of the pails and the clatter of the pony on the flagged yard brought a maidservant to the door. She was pale and fat, her mouth hung down in surprise at the sight of them, and a dish-clout dripped from her hand.

'Who lives here?' called Auntie Robbo, looping the reins over the garden gate. 'Mrs. Van der Post.'

'Oh. Never heard of her.'

Auntie Robbo turned away to look at the garden. Meanwhile Sando was bearing down on the maid with a pail in his hand. She was plainly bewildered, but Sando had begun his patter now, leaning on the doorpost confidentially. She listened in a sort of stupefied wonder. Hector listened too with interest, for he had never heard Sando actually at his selling before. Mary and Pete unloaded more pails hopefully. Auntie Robbo opened the gate and wandered off into the garden. She wanted to see how things grew so far north. Out of the tail of his eye, Hector saw her tall figure stoop once or twice as she looked more closely at a flower or a shrub. She lingered a moment or two beside a white rose bush. She disappeared behind a screen of rhododendrons.

Then suddenly the peaceful Highland scene was rent by an appalling yell - followed by shrieks, one after another, rising in horror and tone, so that the air shrilled and the hills gave back a whistling echo. The pony danced backwards into a pile of pails. Pete and Mary scrambled onto the cart to escape being pinned against the wall. The maid seized hold of Sando, screaming: 'Murder! Murder! The tinkers are murdering the mistress.' Sando yelled too, and kicked to free himself. And into this hullabaloo came Auntie Robbo, galloping madly down the garden path. Her skirts were caught up in one hand, the other pressed her little green hat to her bosom. She made straight for the cart, clutching at Hector in passing. He had been standing petrified in the midst of the uproar, but he ran with Auntie Robbo now, and when she seized the pony's head and forced it round he leaped up on the cart and gathered the reins.

'Get in, get in!' shouted Auntie Robbo to Sando, hopping up herself. Sando hit out manfully at the fat maidservant. But already the pony had crashed forward, kicking pails out of the yard and down the road. Pete and Mary, rolling about in the back, yelled to know what was the matter. Hector would have liked to know too, but this was hardly the moment for explanations, with Auntie Robbo laying into the horse with

the whip and the cart swinging about so that he could hardly keep his seat. He looked back and was relieved to see Sando running after them.

'Wait!' he shouted to Auntie Robbo.

'Can't!' she panted. 'Not now.'

They hurled on down the road, round a corner out of sight of the house, and then the pony began to slow down on rising ground. There was a steep hill ahead of them.

Auntie Robbo flung away the reins and jumped from the cart.

'Come on, Hector,' she cried, making for the bank by the side of the road. The hill bulged up sheer beyond. It was almost a cliff.

Hector thought she must be mad. He sat still staring. The pony stopped. Mary and Pete looked out, open-mouthed.

Auntie Robbo came charging back, wildly impatient.

'Will you come on, Hector? There's sure to be a car following. We must get up that gully - look, to the big rock.' She pointed to where a thread of water fell down the steep hillside. It was overhung with bushes and rocks.

'You two must drive on as fast as you can - three miles, four miles, ten miles - we'll catch you up by night. And when the car stops you, you've never seen us - never heard of us - '

'But why? What's it all about?' asked Pete.

'Merlissa Benck!' hissed Auntie Robbo. 'I met her in the garden.'

Hector shot from his seat as if he had been stung by a wasp. Auntie Robbo had already turned and was clambering up the bank. He raced after her, turning to shout: 'Wait for Sando,' and then he held all his breath for the climb.

It was hard work keeping up with Auntie Robbo. She was going up the burnside like an old grizzled grey monkey up a pole, hanging onto lumps of grass and roots of bracken, changing from one side of the water to the other, climbing rock, slithering in mud. It was a desperate climb; their breath whistled in their throats. Hector's mouth grew salty and he thought his head was going to burst. But at last they reached the big rock that would screen them from the road, and flung themselves down behind it, gasping and sobbing for breath.

Auntie Robbo was the first to recover. 'Not so young as I was,' she panted. 'I've got a terrible stitch. Well, never mind. We're safe here.'

'Was it really *her*?'

Auntie Robbo nodded, and then twisted round to look down on the road below. 'Still there. I wish they'd hurry up and go.'

'They're waiting for Sando.'

'Oh, yes, there he is now.'

The cart looked like a bright toy from that height, and Sando a curious fly investigating it. He ran round to the front of the horse, waving his arms.

'Why don't they *go*?' cried Auntie Robbo angrily.

Actually Sando was demanding that they should go back to collect his pails.

Pete was stubborn. 'We've got to go on like they said.'

'Like they said! Like they said!' Sando spat disgustedly. 'They're my pails, aren't they?'

'Merlissa Benck...' began Mary.

'Merlissa Benck! What's there to be afraid of in Merlissa Benck? I'll soon settle her hash for her. *I want my pails!*'

'Oh, come on, they're all smashed up, anyway...' said his sister.

'That's just it!' cried Sando.

Pete picked up the reins and clicked his teeth at the pony. The cart moved forward.

'Hi, hi, wait for me, can't you? What's your hurry?' Sando had had enough of running in the heat, and scrambled in.

Up on the hillside, Auntie Robbo sighed with relief to see them move off and, drawing in her head, she settled herself comfortably. She sat up very straight with her back propped against the rock, her hands folded on her paunch, and her feet crossed daintily as if she had been in her drawing-room at home. Hector shifted about uneasily. They were sitting on a sort of marsh. Little oily pools bubbled up in their heel marks, and there was a rank sulphurous smell. Auntie Robbo seemed quite impervious to such little discomforts. She tidied her hair, pinned on her hat, and, then, smiling like an old and very knowing goblin, she said: 'I dare say you're dying to know what happened, Hector. What a fuss! I hardly know myself - it happened so quickly. Let me see - I'd been looking at a few things, a white rose bush, and then some rhododendrons - very poor. Neglected. All busy reverting to *ponticum*. Then there was a herbaceous border, really quite beautiful. They had some of these thingy-me-bodies, and lupins - masses of lupins. All different colours - fine flowers. Well, I went up to the lupins - '

Auntie Robbo picked up a stalk of heather and began to chew it vaguely.

'Go on.'

'Well - there was Merlissa Benck in the middle of the lupins. She must have been bending down looking for slugs, I think. She had a big white hat on, and her face was very red. That surprised me. Remember how pale she used to be? I hardly knew her at first. Perhaps it was red with bending - or the shock!' Auntie Robbo chuckled.

'But what did you *do*?'

'Well, what was there to do? As soon as I saw it really was Merlissa Benck, I smiled - I raised my little hat.' Auntie Robbo went through the pantomime. 'I bowed and I said:

'Good afternoon."

'And what did *she* do?'

'Her jaw dropped, just like in a book - click!'

'That would have been her teeth.'

'Oh. Then her mouth opened wider and wider. I saw that she was going to be hysterical. I said: 'Now, now, Miss Benck,' and I put out my hand to give her a soothing pat.'

Auntie Robbo paused. Hector waited anxiously for what was to come next.

'You've heard of people saying that they could have been knocked down by a feather? Merlissa was in that condition. Very odd. And she's not a small woman. Actually I gave her the littlest touch in the world - and over she rolled among the lupins. The bed was quite ruined.'

Hector's face wrinkled with horror. 'And then she screamed?'

Auntie Robbo flung up her hands, laughing: 'And then she screamed! Did you ever hear anything like it? Never try to argue with a screaming woman, Hector. Fling a bucket of water over her. But there was no water within sight, and I thought it might be better just to leave her.'

'Yes, you were quite right,' agreed Hector.

Auntie Robbo beamed with pleasure.

'But, Hector, wasn't it surprising - I mean meeting her again like that?'

'It's terrible. Everywhere we go Merlissa Benck goes too. It's uncanny. She must have a nose like a bloodhound. Are you sure it *was* her? The maid said another name.'

'Van der Post. But of course it was Merlissa Benck. She was probably on a visit. But it *is* uncanny. How could she possibly have tracked us here? We didn't know we were coming ourselves. Or maybe I saw a ghost. Hector, do you think I'm getting so old that I see things that aren't there?'

Hector said no, he didn't think it was that.

'A mirage,' said Auntie Robbo, getting carried away. 'A mirage in the Highland mists.'

'There wasn't any mist.'

'Merlissa Benck has lived in Egypt. She has acquired the faculty of miraging herself - bobbing up in any part of Scotland where we happen to be!'

'Perhaps it was a mirage at Nethermuir!'

'Perhaps she's never left Egypt?'

'Perhaps she's one of the plagues.'

'Perhaps she doesn't exist at all!'

In the midst of this nonsense, they heard the noise of a car on the road below, and hastily looked out from their hiding-place.

A car was speeding along in the direction that Sando and Pete and Mary had taken. It was a green car and had a well-kept look. At the wheel was a woman in a white hat.

They looked at each other gloomily.

'No mirage about that!' whispered Hector.

Auntie Robbo sighed. 'Let's move onto drier ground,' she said.

CHAPTER SIXTEEN

Auntie Robbo and Hector did not venture from their hiding-place till after dark, but they did not have far to walk to catch up with the others. For after Merlissa Benck had stopped the cart and spoken to them and then turned back to her house, they had only gone on another couple of miles out of the glen, and camped by the side of the road where it crested a hill. It was a cold place to camp, but conspicuous, and they kept the fire burning big to guide the travellers. Mary had a hot supper ready for them - potatoes baked in the peaty ash of the fire and a nourishing rabbit broth. When Auntie Robbo and Hector at last arrived, very wearied with their wait on the hillside, it was past midnight. While they ate, Sando and Mary and Pete told them about their encounter with Merlissa Benck. On the whole it seemed to have been a victorious one.

'She was a terrible woman,' said Mary fervently. 'We didn't know what way to deal with her.'

'She stopped the car in front of us,' said Sando, 'and as soon as Pete saw her, he said: 'Holy murder, she's just like my aunt,' and dived into the cart. We were pretty mad being left, Mary and me, but it was a good thing as it turned out, for we told her he was our father, lying dead drunk, and an awful terror of a tinker when roused, and that put the wind up her. And Pete played up. For every time she opened her mouth he groaned and swore and kicked. She was fair frightened in the end.'

'And she wanted to know 'where Miss Sketheway and my stepson have gone?'' Mary mimicked. 'I said I didn't know who Miss Sketheway was but that we'd picked up an old dame on a bicycle that had got a flat tyre, and it was she that set off our horse and bashed our pails and we didn't know what our old man would say when he woke, but he would be pretty mad - probably dangerous.'

Auntie Robbo chuckled with enjoyment. Hector listened open-mouthed - he felt sure he couldn't have thought of such a story in front of Merlissa Benck.

'And what then?'

''Where is this old woman now?' very impatient-like. And Sando said she'd gone back the way we'd come, pedalling like fury on her bicycle, flat tyre and all. 'And the little boy? My poor stepson?' says she, taking out a little hanky and dabbing her eyes. We told her there wasn't any little boy; likely he was dead.'

'You'd have thought she'd have been a bit upset, wouldn't you?' Sando took up the story. 'But not she. She hasn't got any heart, that woman. She just looked proper mad and turned on her heel and went off to her car. We thought that was fine, but back she came. 'Do you go to school?' she said, and I said it was none of her business, and Pete groaned as loud as he could and shook the cart. And that put her off. She really did go away that time.'

'Yes,' said Mary, 'but I heard her when she was going. 'A case for the authorities,' she said, and some more about a 'drunken brute' and 'cruelty to children'. I'm afraid we haven't seen the last of her.'

'I'm afraid not,' sighed Auntie Robbo. 'The only thing to do is to go on as fast as we can. This is a pretty big area and she may find it hard to get on our track. Let's hope she's too busy looking in the other direction for an old woman on a bicycle.'

They slept badly that night, for a draughty knife-like wind bit about the camp, and they were all on edge with thoughts of Merlissa Benck. So they were glad to be on the move as soon as it was light. Blowing on the fire, beating their arms against the cold, bustling about breakfast, they ate hastily off scalding porridge and coffee and got on the road again. The fear of Merlissa Benck drove them eastwards at a great pace that day. They changed roads, too, by taking a hill-track. That was a dreadful business; more than once they had to take the pony out of the shafts and carry the baggage and cart piecemeal over a bad bit of ground. But it was worth it; by night time they'd put a good twenty miles of hill and loch and bog and moor between them and their enemy.

However, the next day all the advantage seemed to be lost; Auntie Robbo went lame with rheumatics. This made her very bad-tempered. They still had to go on, but it was necessarily at a much slower pace. Auntie Robbo lay in the cart wrapped about with blankets and bedding, hugging a paraffin can filled with hot water. This had to be refilled at intervals. In between sips of whisky and lemon and pepper (which she said was the only mixture in the world to cure her rheumatics) she shouted impossible orders at the children. She wanted them to go faster to escape from Merlissa Benck. She wanted them to go slower because the cart bumped her sore bones. She wanted ice for her forehead, and roast chicken for her lunch. She wanted a doctor, and a minister to hear her last words. And the next moment she thought if she got up and walked she might be cured. There was nothing that annoyed Auntie Robbo quite so much as having something wrong with her health.

The children walked along beside the cart, too depressed to run ahead to play as they usually did, and frightened to talk for fear Auntie Robbo might bite their heads off.

It was a relief to everybody when Auntie Robbo gave the order to halt and camp before her bones were bruised to smithereens. They came to a green bight cut out of the heathery hillside that looked a good place to spend the night. There was grass for the pony, a trickle of fresh water, moss to lie on, shelter from the wind. They slid the pony out of the cart, propped the shafts on a ledge of rock. At a little distance they made a fire and their supper - quietly, so as not to disturb the invalid. And at last Auntie Robbo's sepulchral groans grew fainter and fainter, until they were drowned by her peaceful snores. The children edged closer to the fire now, and talked more freely. They were all very worried. They looked at things in the worst possible light, and there seemed to be no escape - the poorhouse for Sando and Pete and Mary, a public school for Hector, and for Auntie Robbo, poor Auntie Robbo, a Highland grave.

'She must be pretty far gone,' said Pete. 'She's delirious. She's never talked that way before.'

'She gets like that,' Hector said. 'I've heard her before. Once at Nethermuir she ate too much syrup pudding -' but he was so near to tears that he could not go on. Shortly they crept away to bed.

They woke to bright sunlight and a well-known voice carolling: 'Ah, wonderful morning! Fine air, dry as a bone!' and there was Auntie Robbo, her hair plastered from a dip in the burn, her face burnished with health and happiness, pulling up heather with the strength of two men, and skipping over the grass with it to feed the fire. Hector resolved for the hundredth time that he would never waste time on worrying about Auntie Robbo again.

'Eggs!' said Auntie Robbo at breakfast. 'Lots of eggs this morning. I'm starving. And two helps of porridge.' And she gave them a lecture on the magic properties of whisky, lemon, and pepper as a cure for the rheumatics.

They set off gaily eastwards again, their faces to the early morning sun. The tops of the hills turned coppery in the bright light, the road was gilded beneath their feet. The pony clip-clopped along smartly, and they ran to keep up with him. The hills seemed to move with them, closing up behind, opening up ahead. Auntie Robbo laughed and joked and sang. She seemed to have forgotten Merlissa Benck. She lingered over lunch because it was pleasant to lie in the sun. And then in the afternoon the hills suddenly opened wide - to undulating fields, cottages, a town, and far away the blue line of the sea.

'Och!' said Auntie Robbo sniffing ecstatically. They all sniffed.

'I think I've got a cold,' said Mary in a small voice.

And then while Auntie Robbo was calling for lemons and pepper and regretting that she had drunk all the whisky - the sky grew dull, the sea disappeared. In half an hour the rain was beginning to fall, in heavy stupid drops, in aggravating patter, and solidly in sheets, curtaining off the rest of the world. It was just like the rain they had fled from in the west.

'Ah, well,' sighed Auntie Robbo, crushing herself into her corner of the cart, 'it just shows that you can't believe much that they teach you in schools. If I was told once when I was young, I was told a hundred times - the west of Scotland is wet and warm, the east coast is cold and dry.'

'That's right,' agreed Sando. 'I mind that bit.'

'Id's cold, anyway,' wheezed Mary.

'Well, it can't be helped. We'll just have to stay here till morning. We will play a nice quiet parlour game. I never liked parlour games, but they have their uses, don't you think - outside parlours? Then we'll have supper - '

'There's no supper,' said Mary. 'What? No supper?'

'You ate all the eggs. I was going to get some more at the first shop we came to.'

Hector said he would walk forward to the town for the supper; he didn't mind getting wet; and Sando said he would

go with him as he wanted to see about replacing his stock of pails.

'Och, more pails!' said Auntie Robbo. 'These everlasting pails! I was just beginning to sleep better o' nights, they used to jangle-dangle so in the wind.'

Sando looked offended, but when Auntie Robbo gave him some money for his pails he forgave her the insult, and Hector and he plunged off through the soaking rain.

Left behind in the cart, Pete and Mary and Auntie Robbo tried to while away the time till the supper should come. They had a long wait of it. First they played paper-and-pencil games until Auntie Robbo dropped her pencil down a crack in the cart and it couldn't be found again. Then Pete began to paint. Auntie Robbo talked about the wonderful climate in New Zealand. Mary sniffed with exasperating regularity. A diversion was caused by Pete upsetting his paint-water over the Primus. It was a troublesome business to mop it up, and Pete quite by accident used Auntie Robbo's green stalking hat. She snatched it from him and wrung it out, very cross, because it was her favourite hat.

When that was all over they went on waiting for their supper. Mary continued to sniff. It was very stuffy in the cart, and very wet when you poked your head outside it. They waited and waited for their supper. It was a most wretched evening. At last Sando and Hector turned up, trudging wet and dismal through the dark.

'No pails,' Sando lamented before they were well in the cart. 'The shops were all shut.'

'Supper?'

'Oh, we got supper all right.'

Sando produced a pulpy package of newspaper from under his jersey. It was lukewarm and greasy. 'Fish and chips,' he said. 'No cooking.'

Auntie Robbo eyed the package balefully. An unpleasant reek of printing ink and vinegar came from it, but she was very hungry and took her share with the rest, though she feared for the effect upon her stomach.

'We got some very good ice cream,' said Hector, 'but it ran in the rain, so we had to eat it. Oh, and chocolate. It's all right.' He produced some sodden bars.

When Sando and Hector had struggled out of their clothes and wrapped themselves in blankets. Mary unrolled the greasy newspaper and dished up the supper. Auntie Robbo melted the sodden chocolate over the Primus, added condensed milk, and everybody agreed the result was very good. After this meal, everything began to look and feel better.

'The sea,' said Pete dreamily. 'I'd like to paint the sea. I'll go and do it tomorrow if it's fine.'

'There's lots of sand,' said Hector. 'White sand and shingle and dunes. We saw from the town. It looked horribly wet. We could bathe if it was fine. You ought to bathe, Mary; it would cure your cold.'

Mary sniffed crossly. There was a trickle of water down her neck from a leak in the canvas, and her nose felt a blob of India-rubber. Hector's remark seemed to her just too silly to reply to.

Hector rolled over and said: 'Shouldn't she?' to Auntie Robbo. His great-grand-aunt lay stretched on her stomach to ease her supper, the stump of candle flickered at her elbow. She was reading the piece of old newspaper that had come wrapped round the fish and chips, and did not reply.

'Shouldn't she?' repeated Hector, prodding her.

Auntie Robbo nodded, swiping at his hand as if it had been a stray fly, and went on reading. The newspaper was a back number of the *Oban Times*. Auntie Robbo read it seriously and intently, column after column, grease spots and all, then tore a little bit out and stowed it under her pillow. She slept that night with a satisfied smile on her wrinkled, weather-beaten face, for she felt at last that she could get the better of Merlissa Benck.

CHAPTER SEVENTEEN

The yellow cart was parked in the lea of a sand-dune. A line of washing flapped across its roof, and near it on a fire of driftwood and seaweed a big pot bubbled. From pot and fire, smells eddied in a warm savoury little tide. The piebald pony wandered hungrily near at hand, nosing the sour, tough bents. North and south, white sand stretched, rimming the sea like the edge of a plate. It was a cold sea, but attractive now in the sun, sparkling and splashed with white where the waves broke. In the curling shallows near the edge three white figures jumped and danced and ducked; their cries mingled with the cries of the sea birds. The three figures were Mary and Sando and Hector.

From the top of a sand-dune above the camp, Pete lay and watched them lazily. He had been trying to paint the sun and

the sands, but he had given that up. It was pleasanter just
to lie. He thought he had never been in such a lovely place
before. The town wasn't far away; he could see grey roofs
and smoke beyond the sand-dunes. Actually they had been
much farther off from towns and people and houses in their
travels in the Highlands. But this was different. Among hills
he had felt shut away but not alone, always thinking that
round the bend there might be a town, or that over in the
next glen there certainly were a few crofts. Here by the sea
there was nothing; nothing to the height of the sky, nothing
to the width of the horizon. It seemed as if only the wind
stalked across the sand-dunes, and only the fish - until Pete
and Mary and Hector chanced along - knew the feel of the
sea. Pete found that very satisfactory. He got up whistling to
put some more wood on the fire, and when the pony came
snuffling up, looking miserable with its nose covered with
sand, he gave it some oats in its bag. And then the loneliness
of the place was broken; away along the shore a motor-horn
blew - parp, p-r-r-rap, parp - and kept on blowing. Pete looked
up. Scooting over the white sand from the town came a large
shining blue car. It grew larger and larger and its horn blew
louder and louder. It wasn't a racing car or a family camping
car. It looked as if it had got onto the beach much against its
better judgment, and the horn had an indignant, outraged
note to it.

Mary and Sando came running out of the sea. Hector
stood still up to his waist in water, and the cold that had
turned his body bright red and stinging, crept into his bones

and heart. For he was sure it was Merlissa Benck.

The car drew up sluggishly in the soft sand below the dunes. Seen at close quarters it was even smarter than one would have supposed; there was a chauffeur at the wheel and curtains at the window and big tassels to pull yourself up from the crimson cushions. A hand gripped one of those tassels now, and the person who had been reclining luxuriously in the back seat, bobbed into view. It was Auntie Robbo.

Auntie Robbo had mysteriously disappeared from the camp after breakfast. She had said nothing to anybody, and nobody had seen her go. Hector had remarked on it, but he knew she would turn up for the next meal. And now here she was - mysteriously come as she had gone.

Whoever would have expected to see Auntie Robbo drive up to the camp in a smart car? - her little green shooting cap (so lately used to mop up Pete's paint-water) tied onto her head in a most professional manner with a long gauzy scarf. Hector could hardly believe his eyes. He waded out of the sea and ran up the beach after Sando and Mary.

Auntie Robbo sat still in the car, beckoning and shouting to them. Pete came leaping down from the sand-dunes.

'Come on,' cried Auntie Robbo. 'Leave everything, come as you are. No, put some clothes on.' The children gaped.

'We're going to Oban.'

'Just for the ride?' ventured Hector.

Auntie Robbo shouted with laughter she was so pleased and excited. 'I've bought an island,' she cried. 'An island, Hector.'

The children began to crowd into the car, asking questions.

'What like is it?'

'What for?'

'Where is it?'

'Who owns the car?'

'What's it called?'

Puddles appeared on the floor, wet sand in heaps; a crab scuttled down a crevice in the crimson cushions. Auntie Robbo's hat got pushed off and icy damp bodies hugged her, but she didn't mind a bit. She chattered as much as anybody else and more enthusiastically.

The chauffeur man turned round and glared at the noise; he was the owner of the car, and he was feeling unkindly towards Auntie Robbo already. She had made him waste his lovely horn so much, blowing it all along an empty deserted beach. And the salt and sand would rot his tyres.

'It's a wonderful place, quite perfect. I saw it the night before last in the fish and chips paper. You remember?' Auntie Robbo produced a greasy paper cutting from her pocket. 'Saw the lawyer yesterday in town. Didn't say anything, in case I disappointed you. But this morning we got it - dirt cheap too, I thought. I mean there's a house on it, furnished, my dears, and a garden and sheep and goats and a boat. The Panther it's called, and it has red sails - I asked the man, or at least reddish, he said - and an engine as well in case we get becalmed - where is it? I really hardly know. In the Minch somewhere. I haven't been able to find it on a map yet. It's so small, I don't think they bother to put it on most maps.'

'How many houses are on it?' asked Sando.

'Oh, none, Sando. None but ours. It's a sort of desert island.'

'But what about my pails?' he cried, thoroughly concerned. 'Who will I sell my pails to?'

But Auntie Robbo and the others had rushed on. 'What's its name?'

'Shanna - I think - yes, Shanna Isle - '

'And how big is it?'

'Five acres. It's really nothing at all, if it was just plain dry land. But an island's different, don't you think?'

'Yes, rather,' said Hector, busy imagining the garden at Nethermuir placed five times end to end and floating in the sea. It really *would* be a pretty big island.

'And it has cliffs and caves and a sandy beach with a little pier. And it has simply millions of sea birds, mostly very rare. We must buy a book about birds. And the goats - did I tell you about the goats? Oh, well, I asked all about it, I can assure you, before I bought it. It's not a pig in a poke. It's an absolutely first-class island.'

'Hurrah,' cried Hector. 'When do we go there?'

'Oh, at once,' said Auntie Robbo. 'This man - such a kind man, so obliging - is going to take us to Oban. We buy a few things. I really must have the skirt of my yachting suit pressed. And then first thing in the morning we hire a boat to take us to Shanna.'

'Is it far?' asked Pete. His eyes sparkled at the answer.

'Oh, miles - that is, sea-miles. Quite out of sight of land, I believe.'

Sando had been waiting hopelessly to get a word in, but at last his opportunity had come. 'What about the pony and cart? Aren't we taking them?'

'Oh, bother,' said Auntie Robbo. 'We'll have to leave it somewhere or sell it. Just when I'm in a hurry to get off. Well, come along. We mustn't sit here all day. I've got my grip to pack too.'

They tumbled out of the car. 'Oh, look how wet it is!' she cried. 'All these pretty plush cushions. I believe sea-water absolutely ruins plush. We must get the man to mop it up.'

She went round to the driving seat, and when she indicated the pools of water the man nodded and touched his cap, but rather sourly. He did not like to say anything, for Auntie Robbo was a most impressive old lady, and it was a good hire all the way to Oban, such a hire as he had never had before and he had been in the business fifteen years. Still it was heart-breaking, all these nasty wet kids, and making him blow his horn so much. When he came to clean up the back of the car, a crab ran up his sleeve. He squashed it grimly. All the way to Oban the smell of crab haunted him, and the way its back had crunched and oozed.

The children had fallen silent, following Auntie Robbo up the beach, partly because they were now very cold, and partly because they were thinking about leaving their well-kept yellow cart and the piebald pony. It did seem queer that they would not sleep under the green canvas that night, or polish the harness again, or run beside the wheels along

narrow roads through the hills. Sando was downright glum.
He had bought three dozen new pails only yesterday.

Auntie Robbo went on talking, noticing nothing. 'Of
course, you know, we have Merlissa Benck to thank for this.
It was she who made me think of it in the first place. But
I haven't given a thought to her since. 'How can I get rid
of that woman?' I was saying to myself when I was reading
that old newspaper. 'She chases us all over the place.' And
there - as if in answer - was the advertisement about Shanna.
I mean the thing to do about witches and bloodhounds - and
I really don't quite know whether Merlissa Benck is the one
or t'other, bit of both probably - is to cross water. Well, we'll
put a good stretch of that between us and her. And then it'll
be our own island. If Merlissa Benck sets foot on it, I'll push
her over the cliff. I've the right to. I've got the title deeds.'

Auntie Robbo saw the pot on the campfire and lifted the lid
in passing. A delicious stew smell rose to her nostrils, and she
forgot about the need for haste and her packing. She fetched
a plate from the cart, helped herself liberally from the pot,
and sat down cross-legged on the ground to eat while the
children were dressing.

'Who do you think will buy our cart?' Mary asked in a
small voice.

Sando could contain himself no longer; he burst out
bitterly: 'I'm no leaving my pails. What are we going to this
old island for? Nobody else goes to it - nobody else lives on
it. And for why? Because it's a desert island and we'll be
marooned, that's all, and have to live on the sheep and the

limpets, and die in the end. It's silly, I think, just when we were getting on so nicely, and I've gone and bought all these new pails.'

Auntie Robbo was staring at him in hurt surprise. The others felt uncomfortable.

'Look, Sando,' said Pete, 'we don't want to meet Merlissa Benck again. We'll be safe from her on the island.'

'I don't care about Merlissa Benck,' said Sando aggressively. 'She's got nothing to do with me.'

'She could put you in the poorhouse.'

'Not she. I'm fifteen and I'm earning my living.'

'Well, she could put *us* in the poorhouse, and she could fairly do for Auntie Robbo and Hector. You surely don't want that to happen?'

'Of course not,' said Sando. 'But I don't want us to die on a desert island either. What is an island, anyway, that you're all so keen on it? Just a bit of land in the middle of a lot of water. I don't see the point of an island. I don't want to go to an island. I want to stay here and live in our nice yellow cart and sell pails and - '

'Well, why not?' said Auntie Robbo calmly and took a mouthful of stew.

Sando's mouth hung open on the tail of his wrathful sentence. The others looked at him uneasily. They thought that perhaps he was only being difficult and really wanted to go to the island as much as they did. They thought that perhaps Auntie Robbo was being unkind in order to bring him to his senses. But they ought to have known Auntie

Robbo and Sando better. They were both as transparent as the day. They always said what they meant.

A broad smile began to light up Sando's face. 'You mean you'll leave me behind?'

'Certainly, if you want.'

'I can keep my pails?'

'Pails, pony, provisions - the whole lot. I'll be very glad for you to have them. It's an excellent plan.'

The others thought so too; it made all the difference leaving the pony and cart to Sando instead of selling it. They settled down to eating stew, now that they were dressed. Only Mary looked unhappy, torn between her desire to go with the rest to the island and to stay with her brother and the yellow cart.

'I'll tell you what,' she said at last to Auntie Robbo, who was lugging her straw case full of clothes from the cart. 'I think I'll come on later. I think I'll bide with Sando - we'll work our way down to Oban. Maybe he'll be tired of selling pails by then. We'll come to the island on a visit.'

Auntie Robbo was sorry to lose Mary too, but she saw that it would be better if Mary stayed, for Sando was a gyte kind of creature to be left on his own.

Now began the bustle of carrying the baggage down the beach and loading it into the car: wicker case, Pete's paints, odd bits of clothing, wet bathing suits, biscuits and fruit to eat on the road, oilskins and southwesters. The driver looked most disgusted at all this junk. He would have liked to have asked Auntie Robbo if she had any money, but somehow he could not summon up the courage. 'Auld tink,' he said between his teeth as he started up the engine, and with a ferocious grinding of gears the car swung round on the sand. Hector and Pete and Auntie Robbo hung out of the windows to wave, crushing the curtains. Sando cheered, waving.

Half-nakedly from the edge of the camp, Mary waved. She looked wistfully after the car as it drove along the beach and out of sight. It seemed a very desolate place now - nothing but sea and shifting skies and the barren sand-dunes.

CHAPTER EIGHTEEN

At Oban there was much to be done in a very few hours, for Auntie Robbo was determined to leave for Shanna Isle as early as possible in the morning. They booked beds in a hotel for the night; they gave orders for Auntie Robbo's sea-going suit to be pressed; they went down to the harbour to hire a boat.

They were directed to the owners of a small fishing vessel, *Leezie Lindsay*, a big red-faced gruff old Highlander called Sam MacDougall and his son Donnie. When Auntie Robbo asked Sam if he would take them to the island tomorrow, he wiped his mouth thoughtfully and then said:

'I was going to the fishing. The ground I was thinking of is in another direction.'

'Oh, well,' said Auntie Robbo, 'we'll have to get someone

else.'

'Wait, wait now. What is your hurry? Where was it you said you were wanting to go?'

'Shanna Isle.'

'Och, yes, Shanna. You are sure it is Shanna you are wanting to go and see?'

'Of course.'

'Now if it was a picnic, there is a very pretty island not so far, and prettier than Shanna - '

'It's not a picnic. I've bought Shanna and I'm going to live on it.'

'Oo - oh!' said Sam, and: 'A-a-ah! You will be another.'

'Another what?'

'Another person, to be sure,' said Sam. 'Well, I will take you in the morning. I will be in a bit of a hurry to get back again. You will not be wanting me and Donnie to land on Shanna?'

Auntie Robbo looked astonished. 'Only to get the baggage off the boat.'

Sam heaved a sigh and seemed much more contented with the transaction. He fixed up time and tide, and advised them where to buy their stores. 'But you will not be wanting much,' he finished confidentially. 'It would just be a waste.'

'Why a waste?'

'A waste of money, to be sure,' and that was all they could get out of him, though he was exceedingly affable by this time. He slipped out of questions like mackerel fry through a herring net.

'Why didn't he want to take us at first?' asked Hector, as they hurried up the pier to the town.

'Oh, it was only his way,' said Auntie Robbo. 'He just wanted to draw us out. All Highlanders are inquisitive.'

'I think he's a wily bird,' said Hector. 'He knew something he didn't want us to know.'

'Nonsense,' said Auntie Robbo. 'Look, there's an oilskin shop. Just what we need.'

But Hector, as they went from shop to shop buying everything that Auntie Robbo deemed necessary for a long stay on Shanna, everything from safety pins to sacks of meal, began to think more and more that there had been something sinister in Sam MacDougall's remarks. For all the shopmen seemed affected in the same way when they were told the visitors were bound for Shanna.

Some shook their heads cannily, others looked shocked or even horror-stricken; some tried to dissuade them from going, while others merely said that they would be back soon, likely. Auntie Robbo persisted in saying that this was just a Highland custom. 'And of course,' she said, 'Shanna's such a lonely place that they would hate to live there themselves. They can't imagine anyone else wanting to.'

Pete agreed with this, and looked forward more than ever to the solitariness of Shanna.

Then they heard that they were not the first owners of Shanna Isle to be seen in Oban; by no means. In fact, already that year it had been bought and sold twice. Auntie Robbo had a qualm at this piece of news, but she would not admit it.

'They were rich English, the last people,' she said. 'You can't expect that sort to appreciate an island.'

But Hector began to feel anxious. He was tired of feeling anxious. Just when everything was going so well! And Auntie Robbo had been behaving so sensibly! Now it looked as if she hadn't been sensible enough. He wondered if it was dangerous to land on Shanna - rocks and whirlpools and so on; or if there was no fresh water on the island, or if the furnished house was damp; or perhaps the whole thing was a swindle - perhaps there was no island at all. After all, they'd never been able to find it on a map yet. However, there was nothing to be done about it now, he felt.

It was about eleven o'clock the next morning when they went down to the harbour. Everybody in Oban seemed to know by this time where they were bound for, and quite a crowd had gathered on the pier-head. It was a merry, interested crowd. There was a lot of talking and laughing going on. But when Hector or Pete or Auntie Robbo walked by them or stood near them, they fell unaccountably silent.

Auntie Robbo was an impressive figure in her navy-blue yachting costume - short skirt, worsted stockings, reefer jacket, and peaked cap. She marched around the pier-head ordering Sam MacDougall about his own boat, commandeering stray fishermen and the harbour master to stow away the stores.

'Where iss your thigh boots, Captain?' called a voice jokingly to her from the crowd.

'In my baggage.' Auntie Robbo replied absent-mindedly.

'Step off that rope, please.'

There was a spluttering of laughter like geese being chased across a field. Auntie Robbo suddenly realized what had been said to her, and lifting her eyebrows in surprise she asked: 'Now why should you want to know that, young man? What a daft question, to be sure.'

The young man hastily retired into the crowd, considerably taken aback - but not so taken aback as Auntie Robbo.

'Extraordinary,' she murmured. 'How did he know about my sea-boots? I only bought them this morning.'

'Och, he was only trying to be funny,' explained Pete. 'Has the condensed milk gone aboard?'

'Yes, I think so. Perhaps we should have got a cow. I wonder if it would be possible...?'

Hector said quickly that they'd be able to get fresh milk from the goats. Auntie Robbo was delighted, for she'd forgotten about them, and she was very partial to goat's milk. She remembered making herself quite sick in Norway from eating too much goat's-milk cheese.

At last everything was ready. The *Leezie Lindsay* was sunk to her gunwales under cargo. Auntie Robbo climbed down the iron ladder to her, followed by Hector and Pete. Sam MacDougall started up the engine, and the ropes were cast off. Donnie fended the pier away with a boat-hook, and they circled out into the harbour. The crowd cheered and waved. The *Leezie Lindsay* slipped through the water - chug-chug-chug-chug went the regular beat of her engine. Pier and crowd receded until the faces became pale discs and then disappeared into the blackness of little figures.

It was a fine fresh morning. They turned their faces to the open sea, which ran strong and blue into the harbour. 'Chug-chug-puff-puff-chug-chug,' went the *Leezie Lindsay* against it, and gurgled when she went too far down into a wave.

Auntie Robbo stood up in the bows like an old Viking, smacking her lips at the salt spray and gulping down the cold wind. It was fifty years since she had sailed in these waters. It seemed like yesterday. She remembered distinctly how they had rammed the buoy at the mouth of Oban harbour - and how Uncle Bertie had put the blame on her because she had been chatting to the helmsman. What a fuss there had been! Uncle Bertie had had to pay for a new buoy; probably that was it they had just passed.

Oban had grown remote now, a mere cluster of grey and whiteness at the foot of the hills. The waves were no longer choppy, respectable-sized lumps of water that hit on the bows with a merry smack - they had become long, slippery tremendous rollers among which the Leezie Lindsay heaved and floundered like a drunk man in a bog. 'Puff-puff,' went the engine, 'puff-puff-puff.'

Behind them Oban disappeared round a jutting headland; cliffs sprang up and receded. They had changed their course and were heading for the long blank horizon. And where was Shanna Isle? Where was Shanna?

Sam MacDougall said it was a long way yet. But Auntie Robbo got out her binoculars, a new pair she had bought that morning. As she adjusted them she muttered to herself, for the first time feeling really angry with the tinker who had stolen her old pair. These modern ones weren't nearly so smart.

For the last five minutes Hector had been listening to Sam and Donnie - they were talking Gaelic. Now Hector knew a little Gaelic, but only a little. At first he listened idly, picking out a word or two. 'Shanna Isle' - 'queer place ' - 'the dead' - 'wicked' - 'poor boy' repeated several times. Hector became curious, but he could not make out more than an occasional phrase.

He reached up and plucked Auntie Robbo's sleeve. 'What are they saying?' he whispered. 'Something about the island.'

Auntie Robbo inclined her head, listening; then burst into the fishermen's conversation with a stream of Gaelic which, if it was not strictly grammatical, conveyed her meaning forcefully enough. Sam looked as if he had been hit over the head with a bottle, and Donnie began to cry. Even Pete, who knew no Gaelic at all, was impressed by Auntie Robbo's speech.

She turned indignantly to Hector: 'They say that Shanna's haunted,' she said, and again began to rate the two fishermen.

Sam MacDougall had recovered himself by this time, and gave as fierce as he got. He complained bitterly of Auntie Robbo's meanness and cunning, sitting there knowing the Gaelic and listening to every word they said without letting on. It was just like a woman, that's what it was, and he had a good mind to turn the *Leezie Lindsay* round about and dump them back in Oban. Auntie Robbo thought it best to apologize, for her Gaelic was running down and she saw she could never get the better of Sam in his own language.

'Well, well, it is no matter. Say no more about it,' said Sam magnificently. And Donnie's tears were dried, and an amiable conversation sprang up about the Highland nurse Morag, whom Auntie Robbo had had when she was young. Sam MacDougall knew all about her brother, the bard Aeneas Mackenzie was his name, and could even sing some of his songs. He was just going to favour the company with one, when Hector, who had been sitting silent, interrupted.

'What did you say about her island being haunted?' he asked.

Sam looked at him with distaste. 'Och,' he said, 'it was nothing at all. It was just a story I was making up to please Donnie.'

'There you are,' said Auntie Robbo briskly. 'I said it was a pack of nonsense. Why couldn't you admit it at once?'

Donnie turned on her in a flash, crying in Gaelic: 'It is not, then, a pack of nonsense. Ask anybody in Oban about the haunting on Shanna. They will tell you the same. And it was us, my father here and myself, that took the last man there. And what happened to him? Yes, yes, everybody would like to know that.'

'Well, what happened to him?' asked Auntie Robbo, and then added: 'Let us go on speaking in this language. I don't want the boy to hear all this - all this rubbish.'

'It was a young foreigner,' said Sam. 'A Frenchman. We landed him on Shanna one day last month. He was going to photograph the birds. Then we went off to the fishing, coming back for him in the evening. He wasn't there.'

'Did you look for him?'

'Certainly. We searched till it grew dark. It was a terrible business.' Sam wiped the sweat off his brow at the memory. 'There's no saying what we didn't see, but there was no sign of him. The ghouls got him.'

'Oh, stuff,' said Auntie Robbo. 'He fell over a cliff.'

Sam and Donnie only shook their heads, disbelieving.

She turned away considerably ruffled; she did not like the idea of a Frenchman having fallen off her island recently: it was very inconsiderate.

'He had no business there,' she added, 'and it serves him right.'

'Would you not be thinking of coming back to Oban with us?' said Sam persuasively.

Auntie Robbo answered him with a single rude epithet in Gaelic. At that moment Pete gave a shout, and stood up pointing excitedly.

'There she is now!' cried Sam, and Auntie Robbo and Hector jumped round. While they had been talking, a squat blue misty shape had sprung up on the horizon. It was as square as a box; Shanna Island looked as high as it was broad, and broad as it was long.

'Isn't it *big*?' breathed Hector.

Auntie Robbo hurriedly adjusted her binoculars.

'It is rock mostly,' said Sam.

Auntie Robbo stood up in the bow, her skirt whipping

about her, her cheeks stung red with spray. She looked long through the glass, making out tall black cliffs, the sea crumbling white against the base of them, a hollow in the land, and in the hollow a white streak that must be the house. She turned, too full of pride to speak, and handed Hector the glasses.

Now they all stared eagerly while the *Leezie Lindsay* crept closer and Shanna became plainer. The glasses went from Hector to Pete, and from Pete to Auntie Robbo, and each could see a little more than the person before. At last there was no need of the glasses, and Shanna rose before them imposing and clear to the naked eye.

It shot out of the sea sheer to a height of two or three hundred feet, solid rock, except on the side facing them where the cliffs lowered abruptly to a green hollow and a little sandy beach. It was in this hollow the house lay, a long low whitewashed building with numerous outhouses and a garden. It looked like a dead seagull, wings outstretched, from that distance.

Half an hour brought the island much nearer, and now 'imposing' was hardly the word to describe it. Shanna was overwhelming at close quarters.

The mighty cliffs looming above them, fissured and pitted with black holes, seemed to be toppling forward to crush their little cockleshell of a boat. And the sea, deep and green as oil silk, swayed and sucked about the feet of these cliffs, growling with hunger, like an old lion who paws a gristly piece of meat and wonders if it's worth a broken tooth and a belly-ache. Even the sea couldn't stomach Shanna.

Flocks of birds fell like snowflakes against the cliff-face, but their cries were smothered in the fuming and frothing of the waves. There was no sign of grass or shrubs; the top of the cliff was naked bald rock. Indeed, Shanna was so exposed that in storms every superfluous living thing got raked and seared off it. Every winter, Sam explained, they got two or three Shanna sheep washed ashore at Oban. But not goats; goats had more sense.

It was a fearsome place, there was no getting away from that. Hector no longer wondered at the remarks of the shopmen in Oban, or the contention of Sam and Donnie that it was haunted by the dead. But he was so awed that he wasn't worried any more; the thing seemed to have passed out of his hands. He had no intention of fighting against Shanna. It was far too big.

'Very picturesque, isn't it?' shouted Auntie Robbo.

'Lovely,' Pete shouted back. He was as pleased as tuppence. This was loneliness for you!

But Hector looked back across the grey sea - the way they had come - and far, far on the horizon, so far that he thought perhaps he imagined it, was the faint smudge of the coast of Scotland. Then he turned again to the tremendous cliff, trying not to feel giddy when he looked at it.

Fortunately there was the little bay and the hollow to break the dourness of Shanna. Nothing could have been more unexpected and charming. They slipped between two outjutting pillars of rock into sheltered water where the waves merely fretted against the white shingly beach. They passed above gently waving weeds and a sandy bottom. The stone slip ran out to meet them, and there was the boathouse at the top of the steps and the comfortable hull of their boat sticking out of it. And behind, a winding well-kept road led up to their house. It was delightful, better than even Auntie Robbo had imagined.

But it didn't seem to appeal to Sam and Donnie. They began to dump the cargo off the *Leezie Lindsay* as if their life depended on it, and when the last box was ashore and Auntie Robbo had paid them their money, they pushed off without more ado.

'It is the tide in Oban we must catch,' said Sam; he meant to reassure them because he felt so sorry for them being left on Shanna, but his voice trembled with fear.

'Put a white flag out if you want us,' advised Donnie. 'We will be seeing it as we pass some day. It is what the others did.'

But Auntie Robbo and Hector and Pete hardly heard, they were so keen to start exploring.

CHAPTER NINETEEN

'This is very nice, very nice indeed,' said Auntie Robbo, stretching her slippered feet to the blaze of peat and driftwood on the hearth. A cup of coffee was at her elbow, and the two boys blinked up at her from the firelit rug. 'I haven't felt so much at home since we left Nethermuir.'

She looked it too. While Hector and Pete had been boiling eggs and opening tins for the supper, Auntie Robbo had washed and brushed and coiffed herself, put on her purple silk taffeta gown and a selection of rings and brooches. It was a long time since she had been able to do this and she enjoyed it thoroughly. Now, with supper over, she was prepared to spend a pleasant evening talking. There was lots to talk about. There was lots to do as well, but Auntie Robbo had had enough of doing for one day. When Hector got up to clear the table, she pulled him down again.

'You know, really this place has all the advantages of civilization and none of the snags. The bathroom, for instance. I'm sure the water heats better than it did at Nethermuir - and no Amy to complain if one left the tap running.'

'And no Amy to do the washing up,' said Hector.

Auntie Robbo laughed. 'That's no miss. But seriously, Hector, what do you think of Shanna? Admit it's a perfect place.'

Hector wrinkled his brows. It was difficult to say what he thought of Shanna. They had done so much since they landed that he hadn't had time to take stock of his impressions. When the boat had gone they had hurried up to the house, and *that* had been the first surprise. Hector did not know what kind of a house he had expected to find, but certainly not like this one. The garden in front, which was enclosed by a dyke and protected additionally by wire netting from the sheep and the goats and the rabbits, was overgrown and weedy, yet well-stocked with this year's vegetables. The currant bushes had been pruned. The gate glistened; it had been newly tarred, and it swung silently on oiled hinges. The house was just in the same state. Though the paint on doors and window frames was worn and whipped, yet the windows themselves were clean with spruce curtains drawn back for a wide view of the sea. There was a geranium in one window, blooming healthily. Auntie Robbo did not have to use her key, for the door was on the latch. It was funny coming into the house - not like coming into an empty house at all. And yet the house was empty, and had been clearly standing so for a long time. The last owners of Shanna must have just walked out one day and never come back. That was Hector's impression. Beds stood ready-made, with the clothes turned down; only they were damp and cobwebs had fallen across some of the clean pillowcases. Cups and saucers stood on the kitchen table as if they had been taken down for a meal. There was a neatly built peat-stack at the back door, and the fires were all laid ready to light. New candles were stuck in the candlesticks, and the lamps were filled and trimmed. But the thing that was really astonishing was the amount of food in the house. The pantry and kitchen presses overflowed with tins and bottles. There was a keg of pickled herring and a flitch of bacon and a salted mutton. The girnel was full.

It was all most convenient, so much so that they had not bothered to unpack their own stuff. When they had lit a fire and set up some of the bedding to air, they set off to explore the rest of the island. That was queer too - but not quite unexpected after what they had seen of it from the sea.

Except for the sheltered cove and valley where the house lay, it was the bleakest, boldest, most unappetizing mass of rock that ever remained above sea-level. It was difficult to imagine what the sheep or goats existed on, for there was only a little rank coarse turf scattered about like mats on the rock. They saw a few sheep on their walk, monstrous ugly creatures, weighed down with unclipped wool, and as wild as tigers. They went racketing away as soon as they saw humans approaching; one dashed clean over the cliff and when they ran to look over, there it was on a ledge at the foot, placidly cropping seaweed. It seemed impossible that it could have got down the cliff face - or that it would ever get up again.

They saw a goat too, a neat spry animal with a broken horn. It wasn't at all afraid of them. It came stalking up, very curious, and then suddenly made a rush forward to butt Auntie Robbo. With a shriek she jumped out of the way and ran for protection behind a rock.

'Go on, Hector,' she cried. 'There's our milk. Take hold of its horn.'

But Hector and Pete contented themselves with throwing stones until the goat tossed its head disdainfully and began to crop some sea-pinks, apparently losing interest in them. They walked on. The goat followed. They had to keep a wary eye on it. Mostly it remained at a respectable distance but sometimes it would creep up unawares, making Auntie Robbo shriek and dodge. Then having walked all round their island, they had returned to the house, wearied by the strong wind, the rushing water, the clamouring birds, and filled with a not altogether pleasant sense of their isolation from the rest of the world.

However, their spirits had risen again when they were within four walls. It was such a friendly, comfortable house. Hector glanced contentedly round the firelit room. The furniture was all well-worn, old-fashioned pieces looking as if they were accustomed to human beings and their weakness, and were very tolerant of them: a moth-eaten carpet, a rocking chair with only one rocker, a solid mahogany table with fat carved legs, a fretwork bookcase full of damp devotional works, a couch with horsehair oozing out of its back; all the residue of a Victorian lumber room.

Hector liked it because it was the kind of furniture he had been brought up with, and he could almost imagine himself back at Nethermuir, safe and comfortable Nethermuir. He remembered how the trees at the foot of the garden there used to thresh in the wind and how he had thought they sounded like the sea: but they were not. Not like this sea at

Shanna, anyway. The sea here seemed to grip the island in its teeth and shake it, growling. It seemed amazing that the things in the room, the pictures and the vases, remained on their perches with so much noise going on outside.

Auntie Robbo broke in on his thoughts. 'Come, Hector how do you like it?'

'It's a queer place,' he said.

'Oh, Hector what a cautious soul you are! Why, if I'd seen twenty islands, and a hundred furnished houses, I couldn't have chosen better.'

Pete nodded agreement.

'This suits me very well,' she nodded complacently round the room. 'And look how clean it is! It only needs a run round with a duster. I'll do that tomorrow.'

'That's just it,' said Hector. 'That's what's odd. It shouldn't be so clean.'

Auntie Robbo was exasperated. 'Of course it's clean. Everything on Shanna is clean. You don't expect any dust to lie around, do you, where even a sheep can't keep its feet? Besides, it's only a matter of weeks since the last owners left.'

'They must have left in an awful hurry. It's queer - '

'There's a thousand good reasons why they might have left in a hurry. Perhaps they had an appendix or an old uncle left them a fortune or their cook gave notice or they got doosed by a goat.'

'I only meant - ' began Hector, trying to stem this flood of eloquence, as Auntie Robbo's voice grew faster and louder and higher. 'You only meant,' she said scathingly, 'that you heard those fat-headed fishermen talk about ghosts - and the queer place is Shanna, ochone, ochone, the meeting place of the dead, to be sure,' she mimicked Sam MacDougall.

'Well, yes,' said Hector.

Auntie Robbo leaped up in a temper.

'Have some more coffee,' suggested Pete pacifically.

'Haven't drunk what I've got.'

'I don't *mind*, because I don't believe in ghosts,' said Hector. 'I only said what I thought because you asked me to. It *is* a queer island. I like it that way.'

Auntie Robbo was slightly mollified.

'What did the fisherman say exactly?' asked Pete. 'I mean, when they were talking to you in Gaelic.'

'A pack of nonsense. I hardly remember what it was all about.' Auntie Robbo poked the fire vigorously.

'Well,' said Pete, 'of course if you say it was a pack of nonsense, it *was* a pack of nonsense, only...'

'Only what?' She looked up sharply.

'Only all I know is that there has been something watching us through the front window for the last half hour.'

There was a stony silence in the room. Auntie Robbo gripped the arms of her chair but did not turn round. Hector looked up quickly at the window. It was blank and black.

'It's gone now,' said Pete, playing with a torn piece of the carpet. 'It had big starey eyes, like electric torches - you know, when the batteries run down.'

'It was the goat,' said Auntie Robbo, not so much suggesting something as stating a fact. 'It was the goat.'

'How could it get into the garden over the dyke and wire?'

'Look how it followed us,' said Auntie Robbo. 'I never saw such a pertinacious animal. Of course we must have left the gate open.'

She got up and went to the front door. Hector got up too.

'Stay where you are, Hector.'

He hesitated; he did not know whether it was worse to stay and hear Auntie Robbo being rent limb from limb or to go and meet the horror himself. But Auntie Robbo marched out without a moment's hesitation, seizing a stick from the lobby with which to smack the goat.

Pete and Hector sat still, every nerve tingling. They looked at each other and then at the black window.

'I don't like it,' whispered Hector.

'Och, it's all right,' Pete whispered in a loud voice, and looked uneasily over his shoulder.

But Auntie Robbo came sweeping into the room, safe and sound. She flung the stick onto the sofa.

'The gate was shut all right,' she said, 'so it couldn't have been the goat. You must have imagined it, Pete, that's all.'

She went and warmed her hands at the fire. 'Let's have a game of cards,' she suggested. 'There's a pack in the kitchen drawer, Hector.'

Hector sauntered out of the room with a candle. But in the kitchen, he whisked over to the table, banged open the drawer, seized the cards, heard a slight noise behind him - the candle dropped with a clatter. Hector fled.

'Here they are!' he cried breathlessly, as he burst into the sitting-room.

'Thank you,' said Auntie Robbo. 'How quick you've been.'

And they settled down to play nap heroically. Soon they were so interested in the game that they didn't need to be heroic at all. But when it came to going to bed, somehow they all remained in the sitting-room.

'I don't think,' said Auntie Robbo at last, 'it would be wise to sleep in these damp sheets tonight. I'll take the sofa, and you two should be quite comfortable on the rug with a few cushions.'

Pete grinned at Hector; but in truth they were both very glad to share such a bed which, though hard, seemed safe.

Hector did not sleep much. Three times he saw Auntie Robbo get up to stoke the fire with peat, and three times on the way back to the sofa, she stopped to peer warily out of the front window. Hector thought that Pete could not be asleep either; he lay so unnaturally still. But when the sky began to lighten, sleep came to them all. They got up about noon, looking black under the eyes and grimy from their contact with the dusty floor.

Pete and Hector went down to the slip to bathe. It was a wonderful morning fresh and sunny; little white clouds chased each other up the sky; the sea danced with light and wave. And when they came to plunge into its green-gold depths above the sandy bottom, it stung clean on their flesh, jostling and slapping them in a most friendly manner. It seemed impossible on such a morning that there could be anything wrong with Shanna.

After a late breakfast of porridge and bacon, they set about clearing up the house under Auntie Robbo's guidance. They aired the bedding and dusted and swept and sorted the stores. They brought up their own baggage from the boathouse and had a good look at their boat. It was rather disconcerting to find how unseaworthy it seemed. It was called the *Panther*, and anything less like its name it would have been hard to imagine, being a pot-bellied heavy kind of yawl. Its engine was red with rust, its paint blistered, and its seams gaping. It did not look the kind of ship in which one could make a quick getaway from Shanna, if that should be necessary. However, they did not say so to each other. Pete said it would be a nice steady easy ship to learn sailing on; Auntie Robbo said it was just the right cut for heavy seas; Hector said nothing, for he had just put his foot through the sail. Afterwards Auntie Robbo did a little weeding in the garden, getting the boys to dispose of the weeds and tie up plants for her. Altogether they had such a busy, useful day that there was no time for exploring or walking or even looking much towards the darker wastes of Shanna. And when the sun began to set, with one accord they hurried into the house for the night.

When supper was cleared away, the cards were got out; but somehow they could not settle down to playing this time. They could not help thinking of the long night ahead, and wondering whether they would have courage to go to their separate beds or whether some excuse might be found again to stay in the sitting-room.

'That's yours, Auntie Robbo,' said Hector, breaking a long

silence.

Auntie Robbo made no move to pick up the trick. She was staring over his head at the front-room window.

He leapt round. 'What is it? Did you see something?'

Pete sat up nervously, dropping his cards.

'It was nothing,' said Auntie Robbo slowly. She began to collect the cards, arranging them neatly in a pack. They forgot the game wasn't finished. Nervously they gathered round the fire. Auntie Robbo held out her rings so that they sparkled in the firelight.

'Perhaps,' she said at last, in an apologetic voice, 'I ought to have been more careful about buying this island. I ought to have made more enquiries.'

The boys were silent.

'We could leave early in the morning in the *Panther*.'

'Oh, we couldn't do that!' cried Pete.

'Why not?'

'Well, we've only just come.'

'Besides, we've never tried sailing the *Panther*,' Hector pointed out. He felt that staying on Shanna would be infinitely safer than going to sea in such a boat.

'I think we ought to go,' said Auntie Robbo heavily. It was so unusual to hear her speak heavily that Hector and Pete both burst out at once.

'It's nothing, it's nothing at all!'

'It's a grand place, Shanna.'

'It's a *beautiful* island.'

'You don't want to leave it yet, Auntie Robbo.'

'Surely you don't think it's haunt - '

But before Hector could finish the fateful word, there came a loud rap on the door.

The three of them jumped from their chairs and stood rigid, listening. The sea hissed and boomed monotonously against the cliffs, the wind whooped sourly once in the chimney, causing their hearts to give an extra sickening lunge. There was no other sound - no footsteps, no rustling in the garden. Most certainly somebody - or something - was standing at their door.

'Come in,' cried Auntie Robbo in a brave, if high-pitched, voice. For a moment nothing happened, and Hector and Pete began to breathe again. Then suddenly the sneck clicked and the door began to open.

Pete and Hector and Auntie Robbo drew together in a huddled group. Auntie Robbo gripped the pack of cards tightly, meaning to throw them over the intruder - whatever it was - and so bewilder it until she could get a more substantial weapon.

And then a face came round the door. It seemed a horrible face, a face in a nightmare - until, sorting it out, they saw that it consisted mainly of horn-rimmed spectacles and a fluffy red beard. A body followed the face, a perfectly respectable body clad in grey flannel trousers and a fisherman's jersey.

'I hope I am not intruding?' And though the red beard waggled uncannily, the voice was gentle and polite.

Auntie Robbo dropped her nervous grip of Hector's arm, and bounded forward with a cry.

'It's the Frenchman!' She kissed and hugged him happily. 'It's the blessed drowned Frenchman!'

CHAPTER TWENTY

The stranger with the red beard and the glasses returned Auntie Robbo's kisses politely, though with evident astonishment. 'Please,' he managed to say at last. 'Please, how did you expect me? And I am not drowned, you know - no, not at all. Not in the least drowned.'

Pete and Hector were still gaping. They were even more astonished than the stranger at Auntie Robbo's behaviour, for they knew absolutely nothing about a Frenchman, drowned or otherwise, who might be on Shanna.

'Permit me to make a small explanation,' said the stranger. 'I am not a Frenchman, I am Swiss.'

'Really?' said Auntie Robbo, forcing him into a seat by the fire, and plying him with coffee and cake. 'How interesting! I've never met any Swiss before - I mean genuine Swiss. I thought they were all tourists - no, what am I saying? Never mind, eat your cake and make yourself at home.'

She stepped back and regarded him benevolently, smiling, like an amateur conjuror who has brought off a trick contrary to all expectations, including his own.

'But who *is* it?' burst out Hector indignantly.

The Swiss looked hurt. 'My name is Jacques Aristide Darabis,' he said, his mouth full of cake.

Auntie Robbo bounded forward enthusiastically and shook hands. 'And mine is Robina Sketheway, Robbo for short. This is Hector and Pete.'

After they had shaken hands, there was another pause while they all looked at each other with growing curiosity. It was such an absurd situation and there was so much to be explained on all sides that nobody quite knew where to begin. And then, as if they had been so many toys wound up and waiting for a spring to be released, they all began to talk at once. Auntie Robbo explained about the fisherman, while Hector explained about the island being haunted. Pete explained about the goat, and the young Swiss explained about himself. Somehow they managed to get to the bottom of the business.

As for Jacques Aristide Darabis, his was a quaint story. He had been sent, two years ago when he was seventeen, to study agriculture at Aberdeen University, because his father wanted him to be a dairy-farmer and because one of his grandmothers had been Scottish. This did not turn out to be a very good plan. For Jacques Aristide, never having been beyond the mountains of Switzerland before, conceived a passion for the sea. He couldn't keep away from it. It filled his thoughts, it sent his blood racing in his veins, it made him imagine things and dream dreams, which he had never done in his life before. When he should have been studying agriculture, he would be down at Aberdeen docks watching the ships come in and the tide go out. He used to go for long expeditions up and down the coast, staying at fishing villages. Then he discovered islands. He visited the Orkney Islands and the Shetlands. By this time the authorities at Aberdeen would not let him study agriculture any more; they said he was only pretending and ought to be a fisherman or a purser instead of a farmer. Jacques Aristide wrote and told his father this, thinking it an excellent idea. But his father was very angry indeed - he didn't see the sense of islands and the sea; he was a thoroughgoing patriot and rejoiced that Switzerland was uncontaminated by such rubbish. He ordered Jacques Aristide to return at once and begin work on the fine dairy-farm he had bought for him; and if he didn't come, he, Jacques Aristide's father, would come and pull him out of Scotland by the scruff of his neck.

When this letter reached Aberdeen, Jacques Aristide had already set forth to make a tour of that delectable wilderness of islands and water - the West of Scotland. The letter caught him up at Oban. It completely upset him. He'd planned that day to visit Shanna. The boat was hired; his lunch was made up; he'd bought a camera to photograph the birds. So, though he was very unhappy, he did not cancel his trip, believing it the last he would ever be able to make.

The minute he set on Shanna, his mood changed. He knew that it was the perfect island, nothing could be more surrounded by water, nothing could be more aloof and inaccessible and altogether charming. He saw the fishing boat move out to sea without a qualm, and set off whistling to explore. He photographed the birds and the seals. He liked the wild sheep. He made friends with the one-horned goat. And in between whiles he refreshed himself by gazing at the sea. Everywhere there was sea, only sea; he breathed sea, the sound of sea filled his ears. Jacques Aristide was utterly content. It was only when he felt hungry, late in the afternoon, that he went down to the house. He thought he might find some berries in the garden to supplement his lunch, and when he found the house all ready for him, so to speak, with food and fuel and beds and water to drink, he had made up his mind at once. He would stay on Shanna. Switzerland and his father and agriculture and all his difficulties faded like a bad dream. As he ate, his thoughts were all of the sea and his island; he planned that in the bad weather he would write a book about sea-birds, so that he could get money for more food and perhaps become famous, which would score off his father. He was very practical, Jacques Aristide.

Then he packed up some food and took some blankets and a coil of rope and hurried to the summit of Shanna again. He had watched the goat climb down to a cave in the cliff-face earlier. And though it looked a difficult climb, he decided it wasn't impossible.

So when the fishermen came back, Jacques Aristide was safely hiding, perched midway between the sea and the sky, smoking peacefully and talking to the gulls. They did not stay long on the island, for the light was failing. They came back the next day - Shanna was soon searched. They did not come back again.

Jacques Aristide lived very happily on Shanna. He did not find it lonely. His day was taken up with climbing and photographing and observing the birds; then he had one of the goats which he milked morning and evening, and he had to keep a sharp look-out for passing boats, always retreating to his cave when they looked as though they might approach the island.

He had been there about a month when Auntie Robbo and Hector and Pete arrived. That completely upset him. He had thought it might be a picnic party come for the day - but, no, he soon found out by watching their movements, by listening at the window in the evening. So there was nothing to do but to fling himself on their mercy, and hope that they would not give him up.

'I will make myself useful. Look, I will weed your garden and milk your goat. I will cook for you - '

'Can you cook?' asked Auntie Robbo. It seemed too good to be true. Already tinned soups and sardines were beginning to pall on her.

'But of course?' cried Jacques Aristide. 'I am a splendid cook - I think nothing of it. It is in the blood. I am born to it. My father is a chef. My brother is a chef. They are all famous.

It was because they did not want any more rivals in the family that they wanted me to be a farmer.'

During the next few days, they found out just how useful Jacques Aristide could be. The island became a different place with him for company. He could climb the cliffs of Shanna almost as nimbly as the sheep, because, of course, he'd been used to mountaineering. And he knew the island from end to end: every rock pool, every clump of wild flowers, almost every bird's nest - and there were myriads of them. He took them to his cave. Auntie Robbo had to be lowered dangling and shrieking at the end of a rope. She had no head for heights, but she admitted that the experience was worth it. He showed them the best place to bathe, and the most sheltered place for lying in the sun. As for his cooking, it was, as he had said, splendid; and there was no end to the delicious and strange dishes he concocted from the island's resources - shellfish soups, seaweed puddings, mutton done with herbs, crab and fish dishes. And he won Auntie Robbo's goodwill forever by making her goat's-milk cheese. 'Better than in Norway,' she declared.

Hector wondered that they could ever have found Shanna Isle sinister, and it became for him and Pete and Auntie Robbo what it already was for Jacques Aristide, the most perfect and charming island in the world.

Jacques Aristide admitted gracefully, after a few days, that far from finding that their company interfered with his happiness, he found them *très aimables*. And then Pete could paint. That was a great excitement for Jacques Aristide. He promptly ordered two dozen coloured plates for his bird book. Accuracy and neatness was what he demanded--and that wasn't Pete's idea of painting at all. Even Auntie Robbo's efforts won more praise from Jacques Aristide at first, though he said that her birds looked as if they were too heavy for their legs, they could never fly. However, Pete persevered; every evening Auntie Robbo and Jacques Aristide sat over him, making him draw lines straight and put in spots without letting the paint run.

And Hector had French lessons.

'Really,' said Auntie Robbo, 'this has been a most instructive and educational tour - what with the Gaelic and selling pails and painting the cart. And now a French conversation with a Swiss! I don't see how even Merlissa Benck could disapprove of us.'

She was well content with her island, as were they all. Only, as Hector carefully pointed out much to Auntie Robbo's disgust, where would they have been if Jacques Aristide hadn't gone along with Shanna?

CHAPTER TWENTY-ONE

Auntie Robbo sat at the door of the house. Hector had thoughtfully carried out the rocking chair after lunch, before going off to the cliff-tops with Jacques Aristide to study the habits of the lesser black-backed gull. Auntie Robbo had fully intended to go with them, but the after-effects of roasted eiderduck done in an inimitable Swiss manner and the rocking chair set so invitingly in the sun had seduced her into taking a lazy afternoon. The sun glared down from a pale, dried-up summer sky, burnishing the wave-tops, baking the Shanna rock, sucking up the sea so that a haze hung like a curtain off the island. But Auntie Robbo felt no more than pleasantly warm, with her head in the shade of the doorway and a sea-wind playing about her ankles. She rocked gently on the one rocker of her chair and blinked at the dazzling

water. On her lap lay a red-covered musty book which she
had taken from the sitting-room. It was called *Good Works
and Golden Opportunities*, and Auntie Robbo knew it well,
for she had been given a copy of it on her fifteenth birthday
and every Sunday for a year she had had to read it aloud
to her Aunt Sibella, who was short-sighted. A sentimental
curiosity had made her take it down from the book-shelf.
But after all she didn't read it. The sun was too bright on
the page and she was thinking she would like to buy some
new clothes, a thing she hadn't done in twenty years. It was
true, her clothes weren't done by any means; built of the
best material, reinforced with padding and lining, whalebone
and stitching, they wouldn't fall to bits for another twenty
years at least. But they were no longer so smart and neat
as Auntie Robbo's fastidiousness demanded. And the goat
had eaten her little green stalking-cap. That had been a real
grief to her. She brooded over this loss for a little. And then it
struck her that perhaps Jacques Aristide could sew as well as
cook - a little mending, a little freshening with a sponge and
a hot iron.... She wondered if there was an iron in their well-
stocked kitchen, but could not be bothered to go and look
at the moment. She dismissed the wardrobe problem from
her mind as settled, stretched like an old cat, and shut her
eyes against the brilliance of the sky. *Good Works and Golden
Opportunities* slipped off her lap onto the flagstones. Auntie
Robbo snored.

Pete was down in the boathouse painting the *Panther*. They
had been busy overhauling her for a whole week, scraping

the bottom, caulking up the seams, and patching the sail, and they were pretty hopeful that they could make something of her yet. Jacques Aristide had undertaken to mend the engine; it now lay all over the boathouse in pieces. Jacques Aristide was still sure he could mend it but the others had become more dubious every day. However, all that Pete and Hector wanted was to make the *Panther* float, and possibly sail, like any other ship; they didn't care much about the engine.

Meanwhile Pete painted in mighty sweeps the curving fat sides of the *Panther*. They had found a store of paint in the boathouse - green and red. It was going to be a noble *Panther* when he had finished; how handsome it would look moored at the slip, green-gold water under its bows and reflected sunlight shifting along its green sides!

There was a faint rattle outside the boathouse. Pete stopped brushing for a moment to listen. The rattle was followed by a queer kind of cough, as if a man cleared his throat cautiously to spit; then there was a squeaking, a lapping of water, a bump. Pete laid his brush across the top of the can. He edged round the *Panther* and peered out from the dim boathouse. And there was a boat drawn up at the slip. It might have dropped out of the sky, for all that he had been aware of its coming. Pete thought he must have been very absorbed in his painting, and he was just going to walk out to meet the visitors when he realized that there *was* something queer about the boat's arrival. All that absence of bustle and excitement which marks the anchoring of even the smallest vessel was deliberate. No one spoke; the crew signalled to each other in stowing the sail and tying the mooring ropes. It was a secret landing!

Pete was puzzled but thrilled. He saw now that the boat was the *Leezie Lindsay* and the two sailors who were behaving so mysteriously were, of course, the owners of it - Sam McDougall and his son Donnie. There were three other people in the boat. The first was a stout little man encased in a pale summer suit; he wore a panama hat from underneath which protruded a black beard, very dense and spade-shaped, which made him look as if he wore a handkerchief mask like a villain in a melodrama. His companion was a woman. Her face was hidden from Pete underneath a wide white hat; she too was stout, salmon pink silk straining at every seam. Pete only glanced at these two, but his eyes remained riveted on the third figure. It was an enormous policeman. Pete naturally distrusted policemen, and this policeman, who came sailing to a remote island on a blazing hot August day with his cap set on straight and his uniform buttoned up neat, certainly looked as if he meant business.

The bearded man jumped neatly as a cat out of the boat and held out his hand to the stout lady. With Sam and Donnie giving a push and a heave from behind, she too landed on the slip. The policeman followed. All this without a word, as if it had been previously planned. Now Pete saw the lady's face and a thrill of horror ran through him from his hair to the soles of his feet, then settled down in the pit of his stomach clammily, so that he thought he was going to be sick. The lady was Merlissa Benck.

Pete had seen Merlissa Benck only once before, through a chink in the canvas covering their cart, but he had never forgotten her - that dead-white face and sandy hair and protruding eyes; and above all the hungry but settled look of an animal about to jump on its prey.

The three walked up the slip. Merlissa Benck hung on the bearded man's arm. The policeman marched behind. He took off his hat to mop his brow but quickly put it on again when Merlissa Benck turned round.

'Constable,' she hissed. Pete could hear the sizzle of saliva distinctly against her false teeth - she was just abreast of the boathouse.

'Here I am, your ladyship.'

'Perhaps you had better stay by the boat after all. I don't trust these Highlanders. They're a most treacherous, sly people. Kindly keep your eye on them.'

The policeman looked sulky: Sam MacDougall was a cousin of his mother's; he was a Highlander himself. But Merlissa Benck chose not to notice this because of his respectable British uniform. He turned on his heel and went back to the boat.

Merlissa Benck simpered up at the bearded man. 'I know I shall be quite safe with you. You will be able to manage this - this difficult situation.'

The black beard waggled confidently. They walked up the road towards the house.

To say that Auntie Robbo was astounded when, wakened by the squeak of the garden gate, she saw the stout, pallid, and relentless form of Merlissa Benck advancing on her, is to underestimate matters. She got the fright of her life. Sleeping in the sun had given her a slight headache; she thought this was a vision; she thought she had slipped into her dotage. It wasn't that Auntie Robbo feared losing her faculties or dying. Years ago, round about seventy, she had accepted such things as inevitable, much as children accept that they will one day be grown up; but by this time she was eighty-one, she had forgotten about dotage and death again, and it was very unpleasant to be confronted by one of them suddenly.

'There she is!' said Merlissa Benck in a cold voice to her companion, indicating Auntie Robbo as if she had been a tree that was to be cut down, or a sheep that was to be slaughtered. 'I hope she isn't going to give any trouble. It would be just like her.'

Auntie Robbo actually smiled; she was so pleased to find she wasn't in her dotage after all.

'Good afternoon, Miss Benck.' She went forward gaily. 'What a surprise! I hardly expected visitors on my remote little island. *So* good of you! Do come and sit down.'

Merlissa Benck was hot and tired and her shoes were too tight. Without thinking, she plumped herself down in the rocking chair. It heeled over abruptly, flinging her into a small bed of nettles.

'Ow!' yelled Merlissa Benck. 'Ouch! Ouch!'

The black-bearded man tried to help her to her feet, full of solaces and apologies. Auntie Robbo cupped her mouth in her hands to stop herself laughing.

'Only one rocker,' she managed to say at last. 'I thought everybody knew. So sorry. Now won't you have some tea? Never touch it myself, but - '

'You see,' cried Merlissa Benck, trembling with rage. 'Always up to these mad tricks! You see how she behaves.'

'But really - ' protested Auntie Robbo.

'I won't listen to you,' cried Merlissa Benck. 'You're not responsible. Let me tell you at once that I have come to get Hector.'

'And I have come for my son.' The bearded man evidently thought it was time to take a hand, and gallantly thrust himself between Auntie Robbo and Hector. 'Let me introduce myself, madam. My name is Darabis, Monsieur Pierre Darabis. Oh, yes, I think you know who I am. The name is not quite strange to you. The good fishermen of Oban thought my son was drowned on this island, but this lady whom I met yesterday morning had a different story to tell. You are a well-known kidnapper. I know all about you. You are not in your right mind and I have a warrant for your arrest. Come now, where are our sons? The game is up - completely, absolutely. Madam, the boat is waiting. It is time to go.'

Merlissa Benck smiled and said admiringly: 'I knew I could trust you, Monsieur Darabis.'

Auntie Robbo wondered if it would be possible to explain the truth to Jacques Aristide's father, and then decided against it. She saw he was a thoroughly deluded man.

'So,' she said, 'so it is all arranged. I suppose you brought a strait jacket for me into the bargain, Miss Benck.'

'Yes, yes, here it is in my beach bag,' cried Merlissa Benck, undreaming of sarcasm. She really was an appallingly stupid woman.

'Well, I suppose I may be allowed a few minutes to pack.' Auntie Robbo turned to go into the house. The black-bearded man followed at once. Merlissa Benck paused to pick up the red-covered book which had fallen from Auntie Robbo's lap, *Good Works and Golden Opportunities*.

'Ach!' said Merlissa Benck indignantly, and flung it from her, then toiled after the others in her tight shoes. Her eyes were narrowed and glistening; she was at the end of a long and weary and expensive chase; the prey could not escape her. The smell of blood was in her nostrils already.

Meanwhile Pete had been sitting in the boathouse thinking. He thought so hard it made his brain hurt. He couldn't imagine who the black-bearded man was, or precisely what Merlissa Benck intended to do. Most likely clap them all into the clink. He wondered if he should try and get away to warn Hector on the cliff-top. But what good would that do? Hector couldn't jump into the sea and swim. No, but he could lie hidden the way Jacques Aristide had done. But that wouldn't work either, for Hector would never stay behind when they'd got Auntie Robbo. And there was no saving her. Not now. It was a mess. Pete fairly sweated in an anguish of thought. Every minute he expected Merlissa Benck to return with her prisoners--and then he would have to go too. Or should he stay on the island with Jacques Aristide? Which would be best?

While he was turning this over in his mind, he took another peep out of the boathouse. The policeman was lolling in the shade of the sail now, his tunic was unbuttoned, his cap lay by his side. He was taking a long drink from a bottle, and when he had finished he passed it on to Donnie. He wiped his mouth and said fervently:

'Och, did you ever see the like of that woman? She ought to have been an inspector. I wish we were well quit of her and back in Oban. I do not care for this business at all.'

His cousin replied with a remark in Gaelic.

'Now, my good man,' said the policeman, mimicking Merlissa Benck, 'have the goodness to speak in a civilized tongue, and confine your remarks to the necessary business of sailing your vessel.' And a fine palaver was going on between her and the bearded chap, and never a word of English in it.'

'What is it all about anyway, Charlie?' asked Sam, passing the bottle back to the policeman.

'That's more than I can say, Sam, my boy. The old woman you were taking across the other week, she was a fine, free-spoken, nice-like woman now.'

'Och, she was all right, eh, Donnie?'

'She would not believe us about the ghosts, though.'

'No, she had a bee in her bonnet about ghosts, you might say.'

The policeman spat into the water. 'What is a bee more or less. You would not say she was a kidnapper now, and had

the children bound and gagged and trussed along with her...
No, I thought not.'

At this point Pete had his inspiration. He slipped out of the
boathouse and down the jetty silently in his bare feet. The
men had their backs to him. He was glad the policeman had
his hat off; it made him look more human.

'Hullo, there!' he called.

'Hullo,' said the policeman, turning round in surprise.
Sam and Donnie grinned and waved in a friendly fashion,
recognizing him.

'How are you?' said Sam. 'Coming aboard?'

'I can't,' said Pete. 'I can't come any closer than this. It's
infectious.'

'What is infectious?'

'Typhoid fever. We got it from the drains.'

'The typhoid! Have mercy on us,' breathed the policeman,
while Donnie squatted down behind the engine as if that
would protect him.

'Well, that's right. Don't you be coming any closer, my
boy,' said Sam hurriedly. He lit his pipe and began to puff
great clouds of smoke round about him.

'I was sent to tell you,' gabbled Pete, 'to go back to Oban at
once. They couldn't come themselves, for the fat lady fainted
when she heard the news and the bearded man is having
hysterics.'

Pete wondered if he had made a mistake, for the
policeman's mouth was stretching open incredulously, and
he was reaching out for his hat.

'Shut your mouth, for the love of God, Charlie,' growled Sam. 'Do you want us all to catch it?'

Pete hurried on. 'You've got to get a doctor. You're to go back to Oban for a doctor.' That made it sound better, and it would get rid of the policeman, for a time at any rate.

He could hardly believe in his luck when Sam demurred at this.

'We cannot bring the doctor back this night. The tide is wrong and it would be very dangerous coming in here in the dark.'

'Well, tomorrow,' said Pete, 'or the next day if you like. There's really no hurry, for we're over the worst of it. I'm all right now, as you can see, except that I'm at the most infectious stage. All the germs are just leaving my body.'

Sam began to cast off the ropes feverishly, and the policeman gave him a hand.

'The doctor's just in case these two silly fools of visitors catch it,' Pete added.

'And I hope they do, I hope they do,' muttered the policeman. 'I was against it from the first. I said no good could come of it.'

The engine spat twice, and then purred placidly. The policeman pushed the *Leezie Lindsay* off the slip, and then as Donnie opened her full out, they went speeding away from the island in a style that would have won a prize at the Oban Regatta.

Pete ran up to the house. He was in time to meet Auntie Robbo and Merlissa Benck and Monsieur Darabis on the doorstep. Auntie Robbo carried her straw suitcase in one hand and her strait jacket over her arm. She had insisted on this, and Merlissa Benck, who would much rather have seen her inside it but was too tired to attempt such a redoubtable task without the help of the big policeman, had given it up with as good a grace as she could. She had remarked in French to Monsieur Darabis that it was best to humour the patient.

When she saw Pete, Auntie Robbo's face lighted up for a moment and then became sombre again. She didn't see what Pete could do. For herself she hadn't been able to formulate any plan beyond a passing notion of shoving Merlissa Benck into the sea when they came to the pier, and drowning her. But she feared for the success of this plan; the gallant gentleman, she was sure, would insist on jumping in to save Merlissa Benck - and then apparently there was a policeman in the offing too. Still it would be very nice to get Merlissa Benck thoroughly wet.

'This is the Edinburgh slum boy,' said Merlissa Benck acidly, pointing to Pete, 'who has been missing from his home for the past three months.'

Auntie Robbo was a little taken aback; Monsieur Darabis raised his hands in horror.

'Ah, le pauvre enfant! Qu'il a dû souffrir!'

Pete looked at Merlissa Benck, and remembering all the things that she had done to Auntie Robbo and Hector, he avenged them to the best of his ability, replying: 'And what a home, kind lady. A fat lot you know about it. Your hat's on squint and your shoes are too tight and your boat's gone and left you. The policeman said he was tired of waiting.' He pointed out to sea where the *Leezie Lindsay* was disappearing into the heat haze.

And Merlissa Benck *did* faint, and the bearded man *did* have hysterics!

CHAPTER TWENTY-TWO

It was late in the evening when Jacques Aristide and Hector came wandering back to the house. They were weary but content; they had had a wonderful day; they were sun-soaked and salt-encrusted and hungry; they carried the little evening pail of goat's milk and a basket of whelks; they were full of information about the lesser black-backed gull.

'Pete should have been with us,' said Jacques Aristide as he pushed open the door. 'Those marks on the wings - ' But he never finished his sentence. The sight that met his eyes in the sitting-room was too astounding. The basket dropped from his hands with a horrid crash, and the whelks went rolling about the floor.

'What's up?' cried Hector, pushing past him.

And then -

'Hector, my lamb!' bleated Merlissa Benck.

'*Mon fils! Mon fils!*' came in deep heart-broken tones from Monsieur Darabis. They would undoubtedly have rushed upon the two boys and swamped them on the spot, but they couldn't. Auntie Robbo and Pete had seen to that. Monsieur Darabis lay on the sofa in the strait jacket, his eyes rolling almost out of his head and his nice black beard looking like the stuffing coming out of an armchair. Merlissa Benck was in the rocking chair, but so trussed with rope and twine and sheets and leather straps that both she and the chair were completely buried. Auntie Robbo's motoring veil had been tied across her mouth as a gag, but she had bitten it through. Her powdered face was furrowed with tears, and a sickly angry flush completed the ruin of her once so perfectly white complexion.

'The old woman is a fiend,' cried Monsieur Darabis fiercely. 'She has the strength of ten men!'

'Set me free, Hector darling,' moaned Merlissa Benck. 'I'm dying.'

Hector and Jacques Aristide stood turned to stone in the doorway.

At that moment Auntie Robbo came bustling in from the kitchen. A towel was tied round her middle and she waved a wooden spoon. Her cheeks glowed with pride and heat. 'You see I can cook if I try, Jacques - only heating up the rabbit stew, but still it's heated to a turn.' She held out the spoon and Jacques, in a sort of dream, licked it. Hector bent down and began to pick up the whelks.

'You were so long,' pursued Auntie Robbo. 'I would have tried my hand at something else, a pie perhaps, only there wasn't time. I fell asleep in the sun,' her voice became plaintive, 'and then all this happened.' She waved her spoon at the helpless forms on couch and rocking chair. 'Such a nuisance.'

'Mad-woman!' Merlissa Benck spat out the word with all the venom she was capable of and a shred of veil as well.

Auntie Robbo tapped her smartly on top of the head with the wooden spoon. Monsieur Darabis said nothing; he had felt the spoon before.

'So come and have supper, my dears. I'm sure you must be famished.' Hector and Jacques Aristide advanced slowly into the room.

'Oh, wait. Hector, this is Monsieur Pierre Darabis - and, Jacques Aristide, this is Hector's stepmother, Merlissa Benck. I'm sure you've heard us mention her.'

Jacques Aristide peered at Merlissa Benck as if she had been some rare kind of sea bird that might bite if he came too close. But Hector passed quickly on, averting his eyes.

'We'll bring you some supper by and by,' said Auntie Robbo blithely to the prisoners, and then added as she shut the door, 'if there's any over.'

Left to themselves, Merlissa Benck and Monsieur Darabis writhed and groaned in their bonds - not so much to get free, that was hopeless, as to ease their aching flesh and the torment of their minds. They did not speak at first, for in truth they were too angry and each blamed the other for the

mess they were in.

From the kitchen came the sound of merry talk, the clatter of forks and knives, and a delicious smell of rabbit stew. Auntie Robbo's laugh pealed out often, and it was often accompanied by the shrill pipe of Hector and Jacques Aristide's immoderate bass. The two in the sitting-room writhed the more.

'What sort of a man do you call yourself?' said Merlissa Benck in a bitter low voice at last. 'Allowing a helpless woman to be tied up like this! You stood by and never lifted a finger. No Englishman would have behaved so basely. How wrong I was to put my trust in a foreigner! No sense of honour, no valour, no elementary - '

'And how wrong I was to trust the imbecile Englishwoman!' cried Monsieur Darabis excitedly. 'Did you not give the enemy the strait jacket? Did you not hand it over with your own hands - those hands I thought so fair and pure and white? Ah, what hypocrites the English are! Do I not know them! You helped her to overpower me - yes, that must have been it. So! It is a plot, a conspiracy.'

'You sot!' retorted Merlissa Benck. 'I was unconscious at the time. I was in a dead faint.'

Monsieur Darabis digested this information in silence and seemed to be softened by it. 'Were you, indeed, dear lady? I was so overcome by the dreadful catastrophe of our boat, I saw nothing, I heard nothing, I knew nothing. The mad-woman had me down in an instant whilst I was distraught with nerves. Oh, but it would not matter if I could only believe that you - that you - '

Merlissa Benck was still very angry, but instinctively she turned her anger from Monsieur Darabis. She felt the conversation was getting interesting. She had not failed to notice that Monsieur Darabis had called her hands 'fair and pure and white.'

'Yes?' she said encouragingly.

At that moment the kitchen door opened and Auntie Robbo was with them again.

'Now,' she said agreeably, 'business first and supper afterwards - if you're good. I have two little documents here which I want you to sign. Shall I read them?'

The prisoners glowered at her.

'Yes,' said Auntie Robbo. 'I will. The first is for you, Merlissa. Do you mind if I call you Merlissa? I feel we have known each other for such a long time - and, in a way, so intimately. Here we are then. Listen carefully. 'I, Merlissa Benck, do hereby see the error of my ways and do repent of molesting, harassing, and generally pursuing my stepson Hector Murdoch and his great-grand-aunt and guardian Robina Sketheway, with intent to abduct the said Hector Murdoch upon whom I have no claim whatsoever, legally or morally. And I swear to forgive them any hurt, intentional or otherwise, which my person or my property may have sustained from the said Robina in my pursuit of the said Hector, and to let bygones be bygones. So help me God.''

'It's blackmail!' cried Merlissa Benck. 'If I have to move heaven and earth, I'll see you in the dock yet, you old harridan.'

'Tut, tut,' said Auntie Robbo. 'That doesn't show a very forgiving spirit. I'm afraid you won't be allowed to sign.'

'I'd die sooner than sign.'

'Well, maybe you will, maybe you will,' Auntie Robbo replied good-humouredly. 'I don't know how long a woman of your age and build can go on sitting trussed up there like an owl without food or drink, but I shouldn't think it would be very long.'

Merlissa Benck burst into tears. Only Monsieur Darabis was moved. 'Merlissa!' he cried out, 'it would be best to sign. You don't want this Hector, he is nothing to you. He is cold, he is unfeeling. See, he is smiling at you in your distress.'

Hector looked up indignantly. He wasn't smiling at all. He had come in quietly and sat down by the fire to be a witness as Auntie Robbo had told him.

Monsieur Darabis continued to plead eloquently. 'Sign the document, Merlissa, sign for my sake. I will take care of you. I too have lost a son, for I will have nothing more to do with him after this, nothing! Let us go away together, you and I, Merlissa, and forget the past.'

Merlissa Benck had long ceased her sobbing. She raised her head now. There was an eager look in her eye. Then she lowered her lashes modestly. She smiled.

'Is this a proposal?' said Auntie Robbo in a surprised tone.

'The lady has just done me the honour of accepting my hand in marriage,' said Monsieur Darabis complacently.

'But she never said anything,' Pete pointed out.

'Yes, that's what I thought,' Auntie Robbo began in bewilderment. 'I mean it may be my lack of experience but - '

Merlissa Benck was smiling now with all her false glistening teeth. 'Kiss me, Robina,' she said simply.

Auntie Robbo backed towards the door in a fright, but then, wanting to make a friendly gesture, she came forward and began to undo Merlissa Benck's bonds.

'It's a trick,' said Jacques Aristide in a cold voice. 'My father only wants to get free. He has been married three times already; his last wife has been dead only six months. He cannot possibly want to get married again.'

His father heaved and struggled in the strait jacket; foam flecked his beard. 'Monster!' he shrieked. 'Cruel, ungrateful son! To think that I came all this way to save you from drowning. Oh, brutal, unfeeling boy! But I have disowned you, already I have disowned you.'

Merlissa Benck's voice now competed in lamentation. 'I have been deceived!' she wept. 'Deceived by a dirty foreigner. Oh! Oh! Oh! Three wives, and one of them not cold in the grave!'

'Merlissa! Hear me, Merlissa! Only let me explain!'

'Hear me!' shouted Auntie Robbo above the din, striding into the middle of the room. 'Now, do be quiet; the pair of you. Wipe your eyes, Merlissa; you look a sight. Oh, sorry. Pete, take your handkerchief and wipe Miss Benck's eyes. Now this thing can be settled as easily as pie if you'll listen to me. Do you, Pierre Darabis, want to marry Merlissa Benck?'

'But of course!'

'And do you, Merlissa Benck, want to marry Pierre Darabis? Now think carefully before you reply, Merlissa. Don't be hasty. He may have had three wives already, but that's perhaps merely his misfortune, not his fault. And after all he's made you a very generous offer. Not many men - I mean - well, in short, do you want to marry him or not?'

Merlissa Benck may have seen the soundness of Auntie Robbo's words, or she may have suddenly remembered her own three dead husbands. At any rate she replied: 'Yes, I think I do,' in a soft, reluctant sort of sigh.

'Well, there you are,' beamed Auntie Robbo. 'All over. That's what's called marriage by declaration. Scots law. Saves times, trouble, and expense. Just draw up another form, please, Jacques, and we'll all witness it.'

'Married?' cried Monsieur Darabis.

'Married?' echoed Merlissa Benck.

'Well and truly married,' said Auntie Robbo. 'But of course you can get it done over again when you reach the mainland if you like.'

A beatific look spread across the faces of the two prisoners.

'Sign here, please, Merlissa,' said Auntie Robbo briskly, and Merlissa signed in a daze the statement which Auntie Robbo had read out to her earlier in the evening.

'And you, Monsieur Darabis. This is a little document saying you won't try to coerce your son into any career distasteful to him, and that you will provide him with an allowance to live on this island till he is twenty-one. Just a matter of form. Sign please... *thank* you. Allow me to help you up, sir. Hector, cut these ropes off Merlissa... There we are. A little stiff! A little cramped! You'll be all right after supper.'

'I don't feel like eating now,' murmured Merlissa Benck. 'I feel so fluttered. Shall we stroll out and look at the moonlight, Pierre?'

'Certainly, *ma chérie*. Love is the food of the gods.' And Auntie Robbo lay back in the rocking chair and laughed and laughed until Pete and Hector and Jacques Aristide threatened to put her in the strait jacket.

The next morning the *Leezie Lindsay* arrived at Shanna, carrying a doctor and two nurses to cope with the outbreak of typhoid. Auntie Robbo had great difficulty in persuading them that the epidemic was all over, and it was only by agreeing that Monsieur and Madame Darabis should spend a fortnight in strict quarantine at Oban that she got the doctor to take these two off the island. *They* knew nothing of this little arrangement, and the parting was of the most amiable on both sides.

'Good-bye.'

'Adieu, adieu.'

'Good-bye, dear Robina. You must visit us in Switzerland.'

'Ah, yes,' replied Auntie Robbo vaguely.

'Good-bye, good-bye.'

The *Leezie Lindsay* moved briskly away from the slip. The four on shore watched her wake widening; they waved dutifully. There seemed to be a bit of an argument going on already between the doctor and Monsieur Darabis, but the boat still kept on its course. They watched until it was a mere speck on the horizon and then turned thankfully away. Pete and Hector ran whooping off to bathe. Jacques Aristide disappeared into the boathouse to tinker with the engine of the *Panther*. And Auntie Robbo went to the house for a little tin pail and, singing tunelessly, climbed up the hill alone to milk the goat. She contemplated her island solitude with great content.

The End

Coming Next...

Firkin & the Grey Gangsters

and other stories

Ann Scott-Moncrieff

Firkin and the Grey Gangsters is a collection of four fabulous tales in which, as with Aesop's, animals tell us more about ourselves than we can.

Firkin is a young red squirrel who has to take part in a battle against a hoard of grey squirrels from America. In 1936, as today, it could be taken as a metaphor for corporate takeover. In the natural world it is of course a battle that continues.

The Sheep who wasn't a Sheep is a philosophic sheep who cannot conform and just be like other sheep.

The White Drake is a farmyard drake who follows his true calling to the wild.

FIRKIN

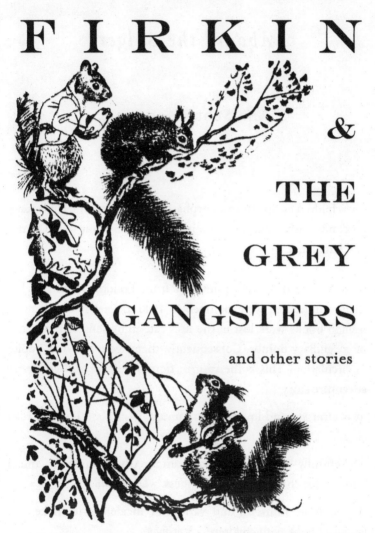

&

THE

GREY

GANGSTERS

and other stories

ANN SCOTT-MONCRIEFF
Illustrated by Rojan

Aboard the Bulger

Ann Scott-Moncrieff

Five children escape from an orphanage. The ship, which in a sense absconds with them, takes them to islands like our own Orkney and Highlands.

The book had a huge print run from London Methuen, but their warehouses were bombed in 1940 in Paternoster Row; 5 million books were lost in the fires caused by tens of thousands of incendiary bombs. Consequently, there were very few copies in circulation. This is the resurrection of a successful children's adventure story.

'It is amusing and inventive and unusual – a good book to read aloud.' - *Observer*

'Delightfully told ... plenty of humour which, unlike so much humour for children, avoids archness.' - *Daily Mail*

'A fine style, humour, and variety of incident will make it a favourite book with children.' - *Scotsman*

'A delightful story with fantasy in the plot but most satisfying realism in the detail.' - *The Yorkshire Post*

ABOARD THE B U L G E R

ANN SCOTT-MONCRIEFF

Illustrated by C L Davidson